After what just happened, there was no way she was staying at the farmhouse.

"I didn't mean to overhear—"

"It's fine. Our father's missing." He rubbed the scruff on his chin and for the first time looked tired.

"I'm so sorry." She got to her feet. "You obviously have to go. Can you recommend a place for me and the baby to stay tonight? I don't want to be here after what happened, and I don't know the area."

"Pack up a few things. You can come home with me and stay at the guesthouse on my family's ranch."

Renee wasn't quite sure she'd heard Cash right. "I'm sorry. What did you just say?"

"You said yourself that it's not safe for you to sleep here. Where else are you going to go with a baby?" Those steel-gray eyes pierced her.

TEXAS KIDNAPPING

USA TODAY Bestselling Author

BARB HAN

All my love to Brandon, Jacob and Tori,
the three great loves of my life.

To Babe, my hero, for being my greatest love and
my place to call home.

Recycling programs
for this product may
not exist in your area.

ISBN-13: 978-1-335-13604-6

Texas Kidnapping

Copyright © 2020 by Barb Han

This edition published by arrangement with Harlequin Books S.A.

For questions and comments about the quality of this book,
please contact us at CustomerService@Harlequin.com.

Harlequin Enterprises ULC
22 Adelaide St. West, 40th Floor
Toronto, Ontario M5H 4E3, Canada
www.Harlequin.com

Printed in U.S.A.

USA TODAY bestselling author **Barb Han** lives in north Texas with her very own hero-worthy husband, three beautiful children, a spunky golden retriever/standard poodle mix and too many books in her to-read pile. In her downtime, she plays video games and spends much of her time on or around a basketball court. She loves interacting with readers and is grateful for their support. You can reach her at barbhan.com.

Books by Barb Han

Harlequin Intrigue

An O'Connor Family Mystery

Texas Kidnapping

Rushing Creek Crime Spree

Cornered at Christmas
Ransom at Christmas
Ambushed at Christmas
What She Did
What She Knew
What She Saw

Crisis: Cattle Barge

Sudden Setup
Endangered Heiress
Texas Grit
Kidnapped at Christmas
Murder and Mistletoe
Bulletproof Christmas

Cattlemen Crime Club

Stockyard Snatching
Delivering Justice
One Tough Texan
Texas-Sized Trouble
Texas Witness
Texas Showdown

Harlequin Intrigue Noir

Atomic Beauty

Visit the Author Profile page at Harlequin.com.

CAST OF CHARACTERS

Renee Smith—Uprooting her life and adopting the baby she's always wanted has put her at risk.

Cash O'Connor—This US marshal has no plans to let anything happen to the new mother and child, and his past won't allow him to become attached to either one.

Jamison Hart—He turned out to be a cheater, but is he ready to let Renee walk out of his life forever?

Kipp McGee—This sketchy lawyer deals outside of the law. Just how far will he go to protect his secrets?

Ms. Hubert—Is she an innocent old woman or tied to a decades-old kidnapping ring?

Darion Figg—Is this creepy contractor fixated on Renee?

Jo-Jo—Did this mover memorize the layout of Renee's new house so he could kidnap her daughter on move day?

Chapter One

The sound of floorboards creaking in the next room shocked Renee Smith out of a deep sleep. She forced her eyes to open, sat upright in bed and searched the unfamiliar dark room. It took a few seconds to get her bearings and for her to realize she was in her new house. She must've dozed off while working on her laptop, which was now tipped on its side. She straightened it, wishing righting her life could be so easy.

The first night in a new home and her new life hadn't exactly gone as planned. Unpacking while taking care of her six-month-old adopted daughter had proved almost comic. The day had been consumed by stumbling through feedings, diaper changings and figuring out parenting in general given this was her first go as a mother. Renee already realized the job was going to be far more difficult than she'd imagined. This had also been the most rewarding day in all of her thirty-two years of life.

That being said, Renee must've been crazy to think that after getting a few months of parenting under her belt it was a good time to change cities. She'd kept her job in order to prove stability to the adoption agency and had started working from home instead. A new life in the old apartment she'd shared with Jamison in Dallas had been out of the question. It was time to move on, figuratively, literally and in every other sense of the word.

The movers had packed up her belongings in a matter of hours. It was the unpacking while caring for a baby that was going to take forever. At this rate, the house might be unpacked by the time Abby went to college. And yet, the small Texas town was exactly the place Renee wanted to bring up her daughter.

She set aside her laptop and pushed to her feet, still half-groggy, and felt around for her glasses. Sleep and being a new mother weren't on speaking terms, let alone friends. The noise was probably just the old house settling but she wanted to check on the baby, whose room was across the hall. Since Renee wasn't completely blind and the glasses must've tumbled off her lap, she could find them in a minute.

A few steps into her walk across the room, another creak-like noise sounded. This time it registered that it might be more than just the wood flooring of her rented two-story farm-house settling. In her half-asleep state, she re-alized that the floors shouldn't make a sound unless someone walked on them. A wave of panic shot through her, quickening her pace. The baby's room had paper-thin walls with only a linen closet in the hallway between them.

A couple of scenarios ran through Renee's mind, her imagination no doubt spiraling out of control. And then she remembered that the temperature had been so beautiful that she'd left the second-story window to her daughter's room open while Abby slept.

But, wait, hadn't she closed that window? Yes, she distinctly remembered closing it, afraid she might nod off. A thump sound from the next room caused another wave of panic.

Was someone inside the house?

First nights in new places were always un-settling, but there was no way this was Renee's imagination running wild. Heart in her throat, she glanced around the small hallway, look-ing for something she could use to scare an in-truder if there was one. An old shotgun that had been left inside the linen closet popped into her thoughts. She'd spotted it during the walk-through yesterday.

She opened the door and grabbed the weapon, checking for ammunition. The gun was ancient, and she seriously doubted it would work even with a shell. The only other weapons she could think of were her kitchen knives and those hadn't been unpacked yet. The shotgun was going to have to do.

Abby cried and that got Renee's feet moving. She ran into the room and then froze. A male figure stood between the crib and the window. He was bent over the crib. She lifted the barrel, aiming the business end at him.

"Stop or I'll shoot," she shouted at the blurry male figure who was picking up her daughter. In the dark it was impossible to see him clearly, even if she'd had her glasses on. Turning on the light could reveal the fact she didn't exactly have a real weapon.

Abby's cries fell silent and for a split second fear shot through Renee that the intruder had done something to her little girl. But Abby was winding up to release an ear-splitting wail.

Renee's heart clenched in her chest. "Put her down. *Now.* Or my contractor will be picking parts of you off my wall when he brings his painter in tomorrow." Talk about making threats with no way to back them up. She could only pray that he wouldn't call her bluff. There was no painter and no contractor, but she sure as hell didn't want him to know it.

Abby was inconsolable. The man seemed to hesitate. Renee cocked the gun.

The next thing she knew, Abby was being set down inside her crib and the intruder was turning tail. She wished she could flip the light switch now so she could get a better look at the kidnapper—kidnapper!—but one look at that shotgun and she could lose all her bargaining power.

The thought of someone sneaking into her house to steal Abby caused Renee's stomach to clench and her hands to shake. Her heart pounded against her ribs so hard she feared he would hear it.

In a fluid motion, he took a couple of steps back and then was out the window a beat later. The second he disappeared, Renee moved toward the window. She withdrew her right foot the minute she planted it because of something sharp. Glass? Had the window been broken? It would explain how the man got in. She checked to make certain he was gone. A blurry figure darted across the lawn and into some kind of vehicle that was too far away for her to make out.

Now that she was safe, she set the shotgun down and moved to her daughter.

"Oh, baby. I'm so sorry. That scary man can't hurt you now." As Renee spoke the words, the weight of them struck. She cradled Abby to her chest and raced to her bedroom in order to check the lock there, needing to be certain that he couldn't surprise her from another room. He'd slipped in and out so easily. Was he familiar with the layout? Someone who'd lived here prior? One of her movers?

There weren't many people who knew she'd moved and there wasn't much to the upstairs. The layout was simple. Two bedrooms, a linen closet and a bathroom with an authentic clawfoot tub was the extent of the space. Renee second-guessed herself for putting the crib in the other bedroom instead of in hers where she could watch over the little girl constantly. A child taken from his or her own bedroom had to be every parent's worst nightmare.

While balancing the crying baby, Renee darted into her bedroom and felt around for her glasses. This time, she kept at it until she felt them. With one hand, she managed to put them on halfway straight. Next, she retrieved her cell phone from the nightstand and checked the lock on the window.

The need to check doors and windows on the first level overrode any other rational thought. She made her way downstairs and checked the front window. There were no other vehicles parked on her street.

Could someone have come through the back

door? Renee ran there, too. She hadn't heard anything else. Of course, it would be next to impossible to hear anything over Abby's wails, the sound of which nearly broke Renee's heart.

She called 911 even though she doubted the dispatcher could hear her. At least the person on the other end of the line would know Renee needed help.

The minute someone answered, she immediately rattled off her name and address. "I'm new in town and someone just broke into my house and tried to kidnap my daughter. Please send someone immediately. He's out of the house but he could come back at any moment and bring friends." The thought made her shudder.

Renee listened for a response. If one came, she couldn't hear it. Abby was so worked up she was starting to choke.

The new life that was supposed to feel like a fresh start seemed to be collapsing around Renee. And she was hanging on by a thread.

US MARSHAL CASH O'CONNOR had had a night for the books. He gripped the steering wheel tighter as he navigated his rental onto the highway heading northbound, home. The felony warrant he'd forced himself out of bed at two o'clock in the morning after a whopping hour and a half

of sleep to serve had gone downhill faster than
an out-of-control skier on his last run.

Not only had the scumbag arms dealer Cash
was trying to pick up in Houston gotten away,
but the jerk had shot up Cash's service vehicle and nearly shot Cash. Traffic was bad on
the I-45, making the drive back to Katy Gulch
take twice as long as it should. Traffic on Texas
highways was becoming as unreliable as spring
thunderstorms. He never knew when they'd
occur or how bad they'd get until the exact moment one struck.

It was late. Cash's stomach growled for the
third time. He was in no mood to stop off for
a bite. All he wanted was to get home to his
log cabin–style house on the O'Connor family
ranch, heat up some brisket to make a sandwich
and have a cold beer. He'd skip the alcohol because he was on call, but that didn't stop him
from wishing he could have one.

Instead, he'd made a pit stop for coffee. He
took a sip. The cup of black coffee from the gas
station that he desperately needed to keep him
awake and alert tasted old and burned and a bit
like what he imagined a sweaty foot might taste
like. Cash figured he had no choice but to work
with what he had, so he took another sip, willing the caffeine to kick in and boost his mood.

To say he'd had a bad day was a lot like saying rattlesnake venom was poisonous.

A few more sips of coffee made it evident the caffeine would do little to combat his exhaustion.

It was early spring. The busiest season on the cattle ranch that his family owned and had operated for decades now. Four generations of O'Connors had worked or were working the Katy Bull Ranch, otherwise known as the KBR. And even though he and four of his brothers had other jobs, most of which were in law enforcement, everyone pitched in this time of year. Sleep was as rare as a unicorn sighting.

Finn O'Connor, the family's patriarch, had always been the epitome of strength and honor and everything good about ranching life. He was a staple in the community of Katy Gulch and used the considerable fortune the family had amassed to benefit others through charitable work mostly headed up by Cash's mother. Folks couldn't help but admire the man's generosity even if they did envy his life.

From an outsider's view, the O'Connors had it easy—easy meaning they were wealthy. But no amount of money could bring back the daughter Margaret O'Connor hadn't seen since the baby last slept in her crib at five months old. The heartache and loss Margaret and Finn endured had shaped the O'Connor family. Tragedy had a way of doing that. It wrote a different history for those affected. One of his brothers, Riggs, worked the ranch full-time. Each brother had a home on the property in a location of his choosing. Each was expected to take his rightful place on the land at some point in the future. For now, their father and Riggs kept business under control. But Pops hadn't been himself lately. There'd been mention of him being ill but he'd reassured the family it was nothing he couldn't handle. Finn O'Connor was made of tough stock. He was a good man and the kind of father most wished they'd had. He'd been married to Cash's mother, Margaret Ann O'Connor, for the last forty-two years. Both sat on top of the O'Connor dynasty because of hard work, honesty and generosity.

Cash had noticed that Pops seemed more tired than usual. Cash chalked it up to springtime on a cattle ranch. He thought about the home that had been built for him as a gift for his twenty-first birthday that he had yet to claim. Most of his five brothers were in the same boat. Six boys. Six future inheritors of one of the largest fortunes in Texas. Not one who wanted either of their parents to die in order to fill a bank account. The O'Connor boys had all done fine in their own right. None were strangers to hard work.

There may have been six O'Connor boys but there'd been seven houses built. A lone home had been built for Cash's only sister, Caroline, a sister he'd never met. Caroline had been kidnapped at five months old and the case had long since gone cold. Even so, their mother had started planning the house on what would have been Caroline's birthday. Just like the others that would follow, the keys had been ready to be handed over exactly one year later. His mother had overseen every last detail, fretting over whether she'd picked out the right color rug for the main room or the perfect pillow sham for the bedroom. Hell, Cash wouldn't even know what a pillow sham was if his mother hadn't spoken about everything during the decorating process. The detailed planning for each home had commenced on each sibling's twentieth birthday. The keys were delivered exactly one year to the day later.

Cash's cell buzzed. With the way his day had gone he couldn't help but wonder *what now?*

As soon as he glanced at his phone and saw his brother's name, Cash pulled off the road and into a convenience store parking lot.

"What's up, bro?" Cash answered before the call rolled into voice mail.

"Where are you?" Colton asked after a perfunctory greeting. Colton was the county's sheriff. A call from him most likely didn't signal good news.

"Getting close to my exit on the highway. Why?" Cash didn't like where this conversation was headed.

"My office just got a call from our town's newest resident on Cherry Street. Seems there was an attempted kidnapping involving her six-month-old daughter. Sounds like you're closer to her street whereas I'm forty minutes away. There are no deputies in the area, either. Any chance you'd be willing to stop off and take the report?" Colton had no idea the day Cash had had.

"This bad guy still in the area?" Cash asked.

"It's a possibility. Dispatch said they could barely make out what Ms. Smith said for a baby's cries," Colton said.

"I got your back." Duty called and duty had always taken a front seat to Cash's personal life. Besides, how much worse could his day get?

There was also something in Colton's voice that didn't sit right. Cash put the phone on Speaker and navigated back onto the highway.

"Everything good with you?" he asked Colton.

"It's Mother. She's probably worrying over nothing." Colton paused a beat. "Pops isn't answering his cell."

"Is he out on the property?"

"I keep reminding her about the dead spots on the property and he'd last been around Hunter's Rock," Colton supplied.

"That place is the worst. I never get service out there." The O'Connor ranch was vast and there were plenty of dead zones when it came to cell service. "Have you noticed that she's been acting weird ever since Pops's checkup last year?"

"I have." Static came through the line, making it sound like Colton was on the move. "She's been keeping Pops on what he jokes is a short leash."

"I had the same thought." Even so, Cash figured their father had gotten winded somewhere out on the property and was taking a minute to rest. It wasn't too surprising that their father hadn't answered any calls, considering all the patches of land with no cell service.

"This time, she's not letting it go. She begged me to put together a team to go out and search for him. That's the real reason for the call. She's worked herself into a panic and I don't think it's a good idea that I leave her alone right now even though she practically tried to shove me out the door."

"Did you call Gayle?" Their neighbor and Mother had been best friends for decades.

"She's on her way now," Colton admitted. "But if there is a kidnapper and he's in the vicinity, you know better than anyone that time is always the enemy when it comes to criminal cases."

"True," Cash agreed. "You stay put. I'll take the call. I'm almost there already. Keep me posted on Pops."

"I will," Colton promised. He supplied the basic details of the complaint.

The two ended the call as Cash pulled in front of 724 Cherry Street.

Cash walked up to the two-story farmhouse, surveying the quiet street for signs of anything out of the ordinary. The suspect might still be lurking, waiting for an opportunity for round two.

No two crime scenes were alike. No two calls the same. Variety was part of the reason Cash loved his job. But attempted kidnappings always made him think of his sister, Caroline.

He white-knuckled his cell phone as he cleared the porch steps, thinking about the impact the crime had had on his parents. It was strange how a ripple could affect so many lives after it was felt.

At least in this case, the kidnapper had failed. Even so, Cash knew firsthand just how much crime changed people, how much it had changed him.

Chapter Two

Cash performed a quick check around the perimeter of the farmhouse on Cherry Street to ensure no intruder lurked around. Dispatch hadn't classified the call as a domestic disturbance. Those could turn into the deadliest calls. He always dreaded domestic cases and traffic stops for his brother Colton, the sheriff.

Standing at the door of the two-story farmhouse with coastal-blue siding and white trim, he heard a baby wailing on the other side. He knocked hard, unsure if the mother could hear. He'd barely lifted his knuckle to tap again when the matching-color wooden door opened enough for him to stare into the palest, bluest eyes. A baby wailed in the overwrought woman's arms, and, although the mother looked frightened, her set jaw and piercing gaze dared him to take one step toward them without identifying himself.

"I'm Marshal O'Connor. You can call me Cash." He immediately produced his government-issued ID. "I was sent by the sheriff to take a report on an attempted kidnapping at this address. Are you Renee Smith?"

"I am." The beautiful redhead examined his badge before opening the door enough for him to enter.

Renee Smith stood at five feet seven inches at his best guess. Her cheeks were flushed on otherwise creamy skin. She had on yoga pants and an oversized T-shirt, and somehow made them look sexy on her long legs and smooth curves. One look at the striking woman stirred an inappropriate attraction. Cash ignored it and refocused on why he was there in the first place.

"I'd offer coffee but—" she glanced down at the crying child in her arms that she gently rocked back and forth "—I can't seem to get her to calm down again let alone…" She flashed those desperate blues at him and his heart clenched. "You came here to take a statement, not hear about my problems."

"Looks like you're in the process of moving in." Cash's mind started running through possible suspects. In cases like these, it usually involved a family member. Based on the boxes, his first assumption was Ms. Smith's husband. He glanced at her ring finger and didn't see a gold band or a tan line. Relief he had no right to own washed over him and that annoying attraction surged.

"That's right. I'm...*we're* new in town." She sniffed and Cash realized she was trying to hide the fact that she'd been crying.

"I'm pretty good with a coffee machine if you point me in the right direction." He did his best not to shout so as not to startle the little one or upset her further. But he needed to get a description of the suspect from the child's mother as soon as possible and he figured making her a cup of brew while she calmed the baby would go a long way toward achieving that goal.

She shook her head like she was turning down his offer. Then she seemed to reconsider as she shot him another distressed look before waving him toward the back of the house. "This way."

Kitchens in farmhouses were reliably both in the back of the house and small. This one didn't disappoint. Even the stove looked like it was from the 1920s. Ms. Smith followed, repositioning the baby in her arms to cradle her up to her shoulder, bouncing the little girl whose cries were pitiful. The homeowner didn't need to tell him where the coffee maker was because it was the only appliance on the counter. He made quick work of fixing a pot while the stressed mother seemed to be pulling out all the stops to soothe the child.

"Does she take a pacifier?" Cash's brother Colton was a single father of twins who'd just turned one. This child was about half their age and Cash remembered his nephews having an awful time with teething.

The leggy redhead shot him an embarrassed look. "I'll be right back."

She disappeared out of the kitchen as Cash checked the opened box stacked on top of half a dozen others. He located a couple of mugs and rinsed them off in the sink.

The crying stopped in the other room. When Ms. Smith returned to the kitchen, she held a tight grip on her child whose eyes were finally closed as she sucked on the plastic miracle.

"I completely forgot about her pacifier." There was so much resignation in her voice. The scene unfolding appeared to be that she'd left her husband, taking their child with her, and he'd come back to claim the little girl and possibly his wife.

Cash filled the mugs with coffee. A small white table, the round kind with flaps, had been pushed up against the wall with two chairs tucked underneath. He set the fresh brew next to her where she'd taken a seat.

"Please, sit down, Mr…" She seemed to draw a blank when trying to remember his name.

"Call me Cash," he reminded her.

"I apologize for the way I answered the door." She motioned across the small table.

Cash thanked her and took a sip of black coffee. This was so much better than the burnt-tasting brew he'd picked up at the convenience store earlier. "Can you tell me exactly what happened tonight, Ms. Smith?"

"You can call me Renee and I'm not married," she said quickly, giving the impression there was a story behind those words. "I fell asleep working on my laptop upstairs. My bedroom is next door to hers. It's a beautiful night so I left the windows cracked. I woke to a sound. I wasn't sure what it was, at first, I mean, I thought I imagined it, or maybe I'd left the TV on. I was so groggy my next thought was the house settling. But then I heard it again and my heart felt like it might burst from my chest."

She stopped as though remembering made her feel like she was experiencing it all over again. A tear streamed down her cheek but she brushed it off with the back of her hand and took a sip of coffee.

Cash focused on the notebook he'd pulled from his front pocket, jotting a few pertinent details.

"What happened next?" He glanced up and realized what a mistake that was. Those sky blue eyes pierced him. They were the color of a perfect summer-morning sky. The kind with white puffy clouds against a blue so soft, so pale, so delicate. Damn if he wasn't waxing poetic.

"I saw him." She visibly shuddered at the memory. "He was standing over her crib. The window was wide open and he was bent over, picking her up." She paused a beat. "A noise scared me. I remembered there was a shotgun in the hall closet. It had no shells in or near it but that was all I had to use. So, when I saw the man standing over my daughter's crib, I pointed it at him and told him to get the hell out of my house."

"What did he look like?" Cash perked up.

"It was dark. I was confused and scared. I'm pretty sure my hands were shaking. I had a tight grip on that weapon. For a split second, I considered turning on the light but quickly thought against it because I didn't want him to see the gun was useless. Plus, honestly, I wasn't sure how it all worked, if he could somehow tell it wasn't loaded. The light from the full moon outside Abby's window made it easy enough to see but he was nothing more than a shadow."

"Can you give me a general idea of height and weight?" Cash asked.

"He was taller than me, so maybe five feet,

nine inches." She looked up and to the right, re-calling facts. "He was medium build from what I could tell. I mean, he wore a hoodie so that's all I could see clearly. I think he had something on his face, too. Maybe a mask. Whatever it was, it was dark and kind of fitted. Shades covered his eyes so I couldn't see the color. Not that I would've been able to anyway at that distance. I think he meant to creep in and out without ever being heard."

"Excuse me for one second. The sheriff is waiting for a description." Cash fished his cell out of his jacket pocket and held it up. He needed to relay the information as soon as possible, however little it was to go on. Katy Gulch's population was fifty-three percent male. This guy had medium height and build which narrowed the field. He had to be young or in great shape in order to scale the fence. He might've known the layout in advance.

Cash texted the information to Colton so he could issue a BOLO to his deputies. He glanced up at Renee. "Who was in the house today?"

"No one except for movers early this morning." She rattled off the name of the moving company. Her gaze narrowed. "There were four of them, but they were pretty big guys. Except for one, he might be a possibility."

"Did he mention his name?"

She shook her head. "He hung toward the back of the group. The crew leader's name was Paul. He did most of the talking."

Checking out the names should be easy enough. After scribbling more notes, Cash needed to take another lap around the grounds in order to get a closer look. "Would you excuse me for one minute? I need to check the perimeter."

"Mind if I come with you?" That fearful look returned to her eyes and it was a gut punch.

"Not at all. Just keep some distance so you don't accidentally disturb evidence." For her sake, he hoped there'd be a clue outside, a footprint or some DNA would give him something to work with.

"I'm sorry. I'm not normally afraid of my own shadow, but I left everything familiar behind to move here and start a new life with my daughter—"

"No apology needed." Cash walked out the back door and noticed she locked it behind them when she followed.

"I picked this town to live in because I believed it was safer than bringing up a child in downtown Dallas. Now, I'm not so sure. And in case you hadn't noticed, I'm new to motherhood," she admitted. "I adopted Abby a little more than a month ago. This is our first night in our new home."

"You said you aren't married. Is there an ex in the picture?" He had to ask the question even though it might come off as insensitive. His job was to investigate, not judge or worry about stepping on toes. Normally, he didn't feel the kick of betrayal in his gut when he asked standard questions.

"Yes, but he has nothing to do with the adoption." Her voice had a musical quality to it even when she was frustrated, like a breeze after a cleansing rain. She added quietly, "I don't need a man in my life to have a family."

"I've met plenty of people who had two parents but still weren't a family." He hoped those words reassured her. He'd made note of the fact that she seemed like she was still finding her way when it came to caring for her daughter. Most seasoned mothers he'd met would've remembered the pacifier first thing if it wasn't time to feed their baby again. The blush to her cheeks when she'd returned after finding her daughter's and then allowing it to soothe her had given her away as a novice.

But the fierceness in her eyes when she'd first opened the door to him also said this woman might be a new mother but she was already bonded to her child. He'd heard about it and seen it with his brother Colton. He'd been hit the day his twins had been born.

It was one of those beautiful Texas nights with a million stars in a sky that seemed to go on forever. And that's where the beauty stopped. As he rounded the corner, he saw that a ladder had been placed against the side of the home that he hadn't noticed when scanning the yard for movement.

"I'm guessing your daughter's room is at the top of the rungs." Cash pointed it out as she followed close behind him near the base.

Her gasp was audible and echoed in the chilly night air.

"That's mine. It was on its side, lying against the house. I should've moved it. All I could think was how handy it would be to have around to paint the shutters and then I promptly forgot it was there." The moon reflected in her wide blue eyes as she stood next to Cash.

He didn't want to notice how beautiful her eyes were in this light. Or how her curly hair was barely contained in the band around it. A few tendrils were loose and he had to clench his fist to stop himself from tucking strands away from her face.

Renee made a move toward it and he knew exactly what she wanted to do.

"Don't touch it. There might be fingerprints

on the metal." Although, he knew that was a stretch. Metal wasn't the best when it came to lifting prints.

"Oh." She stopped cold. "I'm sorry."

"Also, there might be footprints near the base and we might get lucky with a shoe or boot print. You already said it was dark. Any chance you saw what he was wearing on his feet when he climbed out the window?" Cash figured it was worth asking.

"I'm guessing tennis shoes but I didn't get a good look because I didn't have my glasses on." She stared at him blankly. "I'm sorry. It all happened so fast and all I could think about was my daughter. Once he set her down, I was determined to get him out of my house."

"You did a great job. Your daughter is safe with you." Her small smile caused warmth to spread in his chest. Using his phone's flashlight app, he lit the area. There was grass all around the foundation, so no dirt. That would make it more difficult to get an impression.

The glint of metal caught his eye. He moved over to the spot and took a knee. From his pocket, he pulled out a rolled-up plastic glove. He sheathed his right hand and picked up the object. It was a Zippo lighter. The design looked to be a custom job.

Again, a metal object wasn't ideal for picking up fingerprints, but this gave a direction. "Let's hope this gives us a clue as to who tried to take your daughter."

He walked to his rental and pulled out a paper bag. After depositing the evidence inside, he set it on the passenger seat. Next, he closed the door and locked his vehicle. "Mind if I take a look at the inside of your daughter's room?"

"Not at all. Follow me." Renee turned and started toward the house. She unlocked the front door and let them in only to twist the lock once he was inside.

Cash could understand her fear. Being in a new city and a new house with a baby must have Renee feeling vulnerable. The thought was another gut punch. They were racking up today.

He followed the witness up the stairs. The landing area was small. There were two bedrooms, side by side, with a closet in the hallway and a bathroom on the opposite wall, just as she'd described.

Forcing his gaze away from her sweet backside, Cash gave a mental head shake. It was his job to notice things, but he'd never had an issue with professionalism when dealing with a witness.

This wasn't the time to break form despite a draw he hadn't felt in far too long.

Chapter Three

Cash moved around inside the Smith home with a shadow. Renee stayed so close behind if he stopped too fast she'd most likely crash into him. He didn't mind. He was used to it when a witness or victim felt threatened. The closer the person stayed, the more frightened.

The glass in the upstairs window was broken in a U shape around the lock. The perp seemed to know exactly where to go, giving Cash the impression that the intruder might have known the layout of the house. Had the place been cased ahead of time? Cash definitely wanted to interview the movers. He'd worked similar cases where the moving company picked up a day laborer in order to stay on schedule and the person turned out to be a criminal.

"You said this was your first night here. Is that correct, ma'am?" Cash asked his shadow. He'd switched to being formal with her in order to keep himself in check. He shouldn't allow himself to get too comfortable with a witness.

"Yes. And, please, call me Renee. I hear ma'am and I look over my shoulder for my mother," she stated.

The wood flooring creaked underneath Cash's weight. He was considered tall even by Texan standards. He kept in shape. And he was probably one of, if not *the* best shot at the US Marshals office, and that included his brother Blake.

Based on the efficiency of this kidnapper, Cash guessed the person was familiar with the place.

"I've seen all I need to. We can finish up the interview downstairs." He turned to walk out of the bedroom and nearly crashed into Renee. He'd made a point of putting some distance between them to clear his head of her flowery clean scent.

She apologized and smiled. His chest betrayed him by tightening.

This close, Cash had to resist the urge to reach out to the redheaded beauty. He reminded himself why he was there in the first place. His role was investigator. She'd been through a traumatic event and that was most likely the reason he felt such a pull toward her. It was his protector mode kicking in, and nothing more.

He followed her this time, and she led him back to the kitchen.

"Do you mind if I pour another cup of coffee while we finish?" he asked.

"Not at all," she said quickly. Too quickly? Damn, the fear radiating from her. For a split second he mused that he wasn't sure how much of that had to do with the possibility of the perp returning for round two, or if she was scared to be left alone with the child again.

"What agency did you use to adopt your daughter?" Cash took a seat and sipped the fresh brew.

"I used an attorney's office. Branson and Michaels," she supplied. "My lawyer was Kipp McGee."

Cash didn't like hearing that. He jotted down the name. There'd been a lot of questions over the years of questionable adoptions coming out of that law office and with that lawyer in particular. "How'd you find them?"

"Online. Why?" Her brow arched.

"Some of the questions I have to ask might seem personal and I apologize in advance for that. I have to look at every angle and ask—"

She put her hand up as if to say it was okay.

"I understand. Someone broke into my house and tried to take—"

She paused long enough to take in a sharp breath.

"*My daughter.* Ask me whatever you need to in order to find the jerk who tried to take her away from me." There was so much determination in her voice. Her chin jutted out. Her blue eyes stared at him in a dare.

"You mentioned that you're not married. Are you divorced?" He figured he'd better get the biggest ones out of the way.

"No."

"Are you in a relationship?" Cash didn't want to admit how much he wanted to know the answer to this question.

"Not anymore." There was a sharp edge to those words.

"What happened?"

"Do we really have to go into this right…" She looked up at him. "Never mind. I can see that we do and you prepared me for this exact thing. It's just—I'm not really comfortable talking about the details of my personal life to a stranger."

"Again, I apologize," he said and he meant it. Cash never enjoyed this part of an investigation. Serving felony warrants and tracking some of the worst criminals society had to offer were more up his alley, not interviewing witnesses who'd just had their lives turned upside down and sense of safety shaken to the core.

"There's no need. I'm a big girl and you have a job to do." She held her baby close to her chest and he figured her arms must be tired by now. The look on her face said she had no plans to let go.

"You were in a relationship?" he continued.

"Yes. For too long." Her cheeks flushed.

"When did it end?" He took a sip of coffee.

"A couple of months ago. It ended with my partner of seven years getting one of his co-workers pregnant." She flashed angry eyes at Cash. "I know how that sounds and it's worse. He stayed with me in order to save money for the baby they're going to have in two months."

The man sounded like a real prize.

"What's his name?"

"Jamison King." She gasped when Cash wrote it down.

"You don't think…it's not possible that he… is it?"

"Does he fit the description?"

She shook her head. "It was hard to see, though. I'm practically blind without my glasses and he was across a dark room."

"Did you end your relationship in a fight, or did he threaten you in any way?" To Cash's thinking, the man had no clue if he let Renee Smith slip away.

She blew out a breath that almost sounded like a bark. "He said he didn't want the relationship to end this way. But how else could it? We weren't married. We weren't even engaged. He would never discuss having a family."

"What was your reaction when he told you about the other woman and child?" The rim of Cash's coffee mug became very interesting to him as he ran a thumb along it.

"Relief."

"That probably makes me sound like a jerk, but it's true." Talking about Renee's past wasn't as difficult as she thought it would be once she got over the initial shock. It was embarrassing more than anything. The word *relief* had come to her without thinking much about her response. It was weird because she wouldn't have used it at the time but that didn't make it any less true now.

"Not in my book." Cash O'Connor was six feet, four inches of solid muscle. The man practically towered over Renee. His size would be intimidating to most and she figured it came in handy in his line of work. He also had the most beautiful, intense steel-gray eyes and sandy-brown hair—a potent combination.

"I was hurt, too. But I also realized that my feelings for Jamison had changed. I'd wanted to end the relationship last year but then he told me about his mother's diagnosis. We'd been together six years at that point and I didn't feel like I could abandon him or her. Then we found out she was terminal, and I couldn't walk away in good conscience after that. So, I stuck around and played the fool instead. He was sleeping around at the office and I didn't see what was right in front of me."

"Excuse me for saying so but your ex sounds like a class A jerk. Being deceived doesn't make you a fool." His words were low, soothing and provided more comfort than Renee knew how to handle.

But then she was pretty sure anything the handsome marshal said would make her feel better. His voice was like amaretto over ice cream and she could imagine a trail of women a mile long waiting for a chance to hear it. His gorgeous steel-gray eyes were framed by thick black lashes that were masculine. He had that carved-from-granite jawline like the kind that melted resolves. There were so many hard planes and angles to his face. To make matters worse, one look from him sent her heart fluttering, like someone had released a thousand butterflies in her chest. Even though she knew her reaction to him was completely out of place and inappropriate, she couldn't deny it was there.

A guy as attractive as him most likely had someone at home waiting for him. And she was in no place in her life to care how attractive any man was. With a new baby and a new town, Renee's hands were full. And even though she could admit that she hadn't been in love with Jamison in a long time, being burned still hurt. It would be a long time before she could allow herself to trust again.

"Back to your ex. Is it possible he's holding a grudge?" Cash asked.

"Why would he do that?" Jamison had been the one to break off the relationship, if not in words then in actions.

"Jealousy, for one. You've moved on with your life," he pointed out.

"He has a baby on the way with a woman who isn't me." The argument seemed strong until she thought about the hurt look in his eyes when she'd told him there was no going back.

"Believe me when I say that I've seen bigger turnarounds in people. He has a baby on the way but that doesn't mean he wanted it. You said he never talked about having a family with you." His logic made sense.

"That's right. I just assumed he didn't want that with *me*."

"He might not want that at all. He could be planning to leave once the baby's born. You said he stayed with you because he was saving money, right?"

Where was he going with this?

"I did."

"Have you considered the possibility that he stayed because he wanted to?" That question struck a nerve.

"If he wanted to be with me he had a strange way of showing it," she said quickly.

"Did you tell him about the move?" Cash's soothing voice softened the intrusive questions. Even if it didn't, she would do anything to bring justice to a man who'd tried to kidnap Abby, even if it meant relaying personal details of her life to a complete stranger. Renee couldn't think about the kidnapping attempt without involuntarily shivering.

"Hell, no."

"You said the relationship had been over for you for a long time. Do you think it's possible he figured out that you were planning to leave him?" Another good question.

"I guess."

"That could've been the reason for the affair. He might've wanted to make you jealous with her," he said.

"I suppose it's possible." She couldn't imagine anyone doing that to another human being let alone someone she was supposed to love, but when she really thought about it, Jamison hadn't been himself in years. She figured he was slowly losing interest but there could be more to the story.

"I can't rule him out—"

"He doesn't know about my daughter." Renee stared at Cash. "What I do with my life from the day we broke up is none of his business."

"When I speak to him, I'll do my best not to give him any unnecessary details of your current situation," Cash reassured with a look that said he meant every word. "Have you had a fight with anyone recently?"

"Aside from Jamison? There was a co-worker who thought I was trying to sabotage her career when I got promoted instead of her. Her name is Chasity Radar. Oh, and there was a creepy guy at work who cornered me in an elevator recently. His name is Darion Figg and he's a contractor. I told my boss, who immediately handled it."

"What's your boss's name and what's your profession?"

"Rikki Drake. I handle all the updates for my company's website." She supplied her contact number. Rikki needed a heads-up and she figured this wasn't a quick email or text. She owed her a call if a US marshal would be contacting her boss.

"What about your family? Do you have any family nearby?" he asked, and it was another painful question.

"No. That was part of the appeal in moving here," she admitted. "My parents used to live in Dallas."

He rocked his head as he took notes.

"We didn't see eye to eye on much, I'm afraid. But they've been gone a long time." Renee wished she'd been on better terms with her parents. "They fought a lot while I was growing up. They died in a car crash."

"Shame," he said almost under his breath. "I'm sorry for your loss and I'm sorry their relationship was strained."

"Why is that?" She cocked her head to one side, curious. He seemed genuinely sad for her and her nonexistent relationship with her folks. It was pretty much all she'd ever known, so it didn't seem as strange to her as it appeared it did to him.

"I grew up close to mine. My whole family is there for each other. Hard to imagine life any other way even though I see it every day in my line of work." There was a sincerity to his steel eyes that pierced her armor and hit straight in the chest where it exploded. Renee had no idea what it was like for someone else to have her back. It had just been her for longer than she cared to remember. She'd been the only child of parents who thought shouting at each other and being violent should be a professional sport.

"You have brothers and sisters?" she asked, curious about the mysterious marshal.

"Five brothers." An emotion flickered behind his eyes that she couldn't quite pinpoint. Then came, "We had a sister."

"I'm sorry for your loss." Without thinking, she reached across the table and touched his arm. It was intended to reassure him but contact sent a fire bolt of electricity shooting up her arm.

If he had the same reaction he didn't show it. Instead, he nodded his appreciation for the sentiment and took another sip of coffee.

"Any fights about money with your ex?" he continued.

"No. He mainly didn't seem thrilled that I kicked him out or wouldn't take his calls, but I wouldn't exactly say we had a fight. I guess a breakup in and of itself is never pleasant," she said.

"None I've ever been part of ended without someone's feelings being hurt." One corner of his mouth lifted when he spoke. She liked his face even more when he relaxed. "You mentioned the movers before. Did any friends drop by?"

"A neighbor grabbed me to say hello, but I had my hands full with Abby so I didn't invite her inside." A shiver raced down her back at the thought that one of the people she'd hired could've been a criminal who was casing the place.

"We can start with the movers, then." He picked up his pen. "Do you have any documentation from the moving company?"

"I have the receipt right here." She sifted through a couple of papers on the table and located the pink slip for College Boy Movers. The slogan had been College Hunks Move Your Stuff. The guys who'd shown up wouldn't exactly fall into the category of good-looking. Three slightly overweight men and a slightly smaller one in their late twenties had turned up at her Dallas apartment to get the job done. "They put together Abby's crib, so one of the guys was in her room. It was part of the deal. They helped set the place up. They don't unpack necessarily, but they were handy with a screwdriver and got my bed put back together."

They might not have been a good-looking crew but they got the job done well enough. Renee was in her new home.

Cash took the slip and studied it.

"Have you heard of them?" she asked.

"No. And that's a good thing from my perspective." He glanced up. "Mind if I take a picture of this to file with my report?"

The question was most likely professional courtesy. She shook her head and suppressed a yawn. He asked a few more routine-sounding questions before snapping a pic. His cell buzzed while still in his hand.

He glanced at the screen. "Excuse me, I need to take this."

"Go right ahead." She glanced at the clock. It was getting late. Exhaustion wore her thin but she doubted she could go back to sleep, especially now that she realized the glass had been broken in her daughter's room and there was no way to lock the window. Maybe she could pack an overnight bag and stay in a motel until she could have her new home secured. She needed a temporary fix tonight.

Cash stood and walked over to the sink, looking out the window. "Hey, Colton. What's the word?"

She surmised the call must be from the sheriff. And then it dawned on her. Her neighbor had said the sheriff's name was Colton O'Connor. He had the same last name as Cash, who'd said he had five brothers.

Renee wouldn't normally listen to someone's

conversation, but she figured this one had to do with her as she heard Cash update his brother on the case and tell him about the lighter he'd found.

After saying a few uh-huhs into the phone and promising to run the evidence to his brother's office, the conversation must've shifted to something more personal.

"And no one's seen him?" he asked, with concern in his voice.

Suddenly, she felt like she was intruding. She stared down at her little girl and tried to block out the sound of his voice, which was difficult to do with the way it seemed to tickle her skin like the first cool breeze on a hot day.

"Where was it found?" His voice went silent. "I see."

More silence.

"And how's Mother taking the news—don't answer that. Stupid question." He was silent for a couple of beats. "He wouldn't part from his cell phone. The entire area has been checked? And nothing? It's still dark outside. It'll be difficult to find him now. He knows the area like the back of his hand. There's no way he's lost." Cash gripped the sink with his free hand as though he was bracing himself. He bowed his head and closed his eyes. "I need to finish boarding up the window at the victim's home. Since you're sending a deputy here to collect evidence, I'll wait until he's finished. After that, I'm on my way home."

Renee's heart was in her throat. She was scared and too stubborn to admit her fears. Cash said goodbye before ending the call. Maybe strapping the baby in the car seat and getting a hotel room was a good idea after all. But where?

An idea popped. She should ask the lawman for a recommendation. He'd know the area, and until the window was fixed there was no way she was staying at the farmhouse.

"I didn't mean to overhear—"

"It's fine. Our father's missing." He rubbed the scruff on his chin and for the first time looked tired.

"I'm so sorry." She got to her feet. "You obviously have to go. Can you recommend a place for me and the baby to stay tonight? I don't want to be here after what happened and I don't know the area."

"Pack up a few things. You can come home with me and stay at the guesthouse on my family's ranch."

Renee wasn't quite sure she'd heard Cash right. "I'm sorry. What did you just say?"

"You said yourself that it's not safe for you to sleep here. Where else are you going to go with a baby?" Those steel-gray eyes pierced her.

Well, when he put it like that it didn't sound so crazy. But she didn't know the man. "Thanks for the offer—"

"This is a practical solution. Besides, I don't know how long we'll be searching for my father. Everyone around here and in town knows who he is and people will most likely storm the ranch to help find him until he comes home or is found. I can't leave you and your daughter unprotected. There's a motel about twenty miles from here on the highway, but I'm pretty certain they rent rooms by the hour."

She must've made an awful face because he said, "That's exactly right. So, I'd like you to come to my family's ranch. We're good people. Several of my brothers and I work in law enforcement. The ranch has everything you could possibly need and you'll be safe until we can arrest the jerk who broke into your house or get a permanent solution for your window and install an alarm. Think about it while I board up the window in the baby's room. My brother is sending a deputy to gather evidence."

He glanced around.

"Any chance you have supplies anywhere around?" he asked.

"There's a shed in back."

She followed him outside, locking the door

behind them. He found a few supplies in the shed and then brought them into the house.

Renee wouldn't normally agree to stay at a stranger's house. She glanced down at her now-sleeping angel and then back at Cash several times as he worked. Because of him, her daughter was calm and sleeping. His job was to enforce the law. His family owned a ranch with plenty of room and, apparently, a guesthouse.

A few warning flares fired when she looked at that man because she'd never felt an attraction this fast and hard, or this strong. But this was the best plan to keep her daughter safe for the night until Renee could get someone over to repair the window and put in an alarm.

Renee could scarcely believe she was about to accept an invitation to stay with a practical stranger. The "old" her might have dug her heels in and tried to stick it out for the night in the new house just to prove a point. There was never a doubt in her mind having a baby would change her. She figured this was just the tip of the iceberg. Abby would always come first. Renee's pride would gladly take a back seat to ensure her child's safety.

It didn't take him more than ten minutes to hammer in a few nails and secure the bedroom. The deputy arrived while Cash worked and dusted for prints. He took the evidence that had been collected so far before thanking Cash and expressing concern for his father.

Once they'd seen the deputy out, Cash put the hammer down in the hall closet before turning toward her and asking, "Have you made a decision?"

"Thank you for the invite," she said to Cash. "I accept."

Chapter Four

Renee's eyes widened as Cash pulled onto the paved driveway of a massive ranch after a forty-minute drive. Even this early in the morning, the place was well lit. It was huge and grand and completely unexpected.

After being waved in by a security guard, Cash continued onto a paved road toward a massive white house. Before they got anywhere close, Cash turned onto a smaller road.

"The guesthouse is this way. The opposite direction leads to the barns where Pops keeps his offices. There's a bunkhouse over that way." His tone was much more somber now, his concern for his father evident. The emotion hit Renee harder than she wanted it to. All she could think was how much she respected his family for being so close. "Stacy is my parents' right hand."

"Was she the person you called before we left my house?" The forty-minute drive to the ranch went by in a flash with a sleeping baby buckled in her carrier that doubled as a car seat. Conversation had been light and interrupted often by calls from Cash's brothers that came over the speaker.

Cash nodded. "She made sure you'll have all the supplies you need for your little one. Fridge is stocked."

"She did all that in forty minutes?" Renee had packed up bottles and formula along with an overnight bag for herself. Feeding time should hit soon.

Looking down, she realized she'd fisted her hands. She flexed her fingers, trying to release some of the tension of being in new territory and feeling ill-equipped to handle it. None of this felt great but every day spent figuring life out on her own was going to be better than the last few years with Jamison.

"This place runs like a well-oiled machine because of the team my parents put in place. I have a cabin—"

"Hold on a minute. You're not staying the night in the guesthouse with us?" Renee wasn't trying to be forward or take Cash for granted. He was the only person she knew in the whole town.

"I'd planned to join the search for my father."

"Oh, right. I'm sorry." She pinched the bridge of her nose to stave off the raging headache forming along with a very real dose of fear that this motherhood gig might be biting off more than she could chew. Renee took in a breath and mentally shook off the negativity. She'd figure this out with Abby. No one could possibly want to do a better job at being a mother than her.

"I can send someone over to help until I get back after we find him." Those last few spoken words faltered. He tried to hide his emotions by clearing his throat.

"Providing us with a safe roof over our heads for a day or two until we can get everything straightened out at home is more than enough." The idea of an extra set of hands and possibly someone with experience caring for a child was almost too good to pass up, but she didn't want to impose. He was doing more than enough for her makeshift family as it was. And he'd received unsettling news about his father.

"It's no trouble and you might be able to get a few hours of shut-eye."

She was already shaking her head before he finished his sentence. There was no way she would ask that of him, no matter how tempting the offer. Abby needed stability in her life and that came with having a consistent caregiver. Renee was more than ready for the job and had been getting by okay for the past month despite plenty of moments that might make her feel otherwise.

"I'll manage okay. I have to get used to lack of sleep and taking care of her on my own, right? It might be scary but it's also the best job I've ever had." Her half smile was rewarded with a chuckle that sounded like a deep rumble from his chest. "Thank you, though. Your hospitality is above and beyond. It's more than appreciated."

"Your 'welcome to town' up to this point hasn't exactly been stellar. I'm hoping you'll see we aren't all bad." His cell had been buzzing like crazy for the past twenty minutes or so. He parked in front of a cottage and palmed his cell. "It's a one-bedroom but the rooms are good size."

Before she could unbuckle her seat belt, he'd exited the vehicle and come around to her side. As she reached for the handle, the door opened. Turned out, chivalry wasn't dead. Jamison had never displayed this kind of southern charm despite being from a Dallas suburb. She thanked him again as she climbed out of the seat.

Cash was already liberating the car seat from the buckle in back. Did he have a family? He seemed to know his way around children. Of course, a man as intelligent and hot as him would have someone waiting at home. Was that the reason he'd taken her to the guesthouse instead of his place?

"I hope I don't get you in any trouble with your wife—"

"No wife." Those two words were spoken with a finiteness that came with careful contemplation and a decision. Maybe he wasn't the marrying type. Plenty of people staked a claim on being single.

"Oh. Okay. Just don't let me keep you." Renee had always known she wanted a family. Despite her parents' endless arguments, she'd convinced herself that she would somehow magically get marriage right. She'd worked briefly at a preschool while finishing her basics at community college and loved the energy of having lots of little kids around.

Jamison was no doubt the wrong person for her but her confidence in finding the "right" person took a huge hit after everything that happened with him. After learning about his betrayal, marriage didn't seem like the best requirement for starting a family. He'd been reaching out to her a lot recently and getting frustrated with her lack of response to his frequent texts. What could she say? She was done. He had a baby on the way. He might regret his choices but his actions had consequences.

"I've got her. You want to grab the diaper

bag?" Cash asked. "I can come back for the suitcase once you're settled."

"Yeah, sure." She couldn't help but notice the ease with which he handled her daughter. Curiosity got the best of her. "You're not married, which doesn't necessarily mean you don't have kids."

He laughed as he balanced the carrier in one arm and slid the key in the lock with his free hand. The door opened and he flipped on a light. "I have nephews. A set of twin boys who just celebrated their first birthday. I've learned to pitch in to help my brother. He's raising them on his own." He shot her a warning look. It wasn't so much the words as the way he'd said them that told her more discussion of the topic was off limits.

Changing the subject seemed like a good idea as Abby stirred. She had to be hungry by now. "You can put her down anywhere. I need to get a bottle ready."

True to form, the fridge had all the basics of milk, eggs and a couple of what looked like precooked homemade meals in ready-to-heat containers. She was even more impressed. The interior of the cottage was beige and white with just enough Tiffany blue to be considered feminine. The place was decorated to perfection, looking like something out of a magazine. She should've expected this but for some reason was surprised by the level of detail.

"It's beautiful in here." She set the bottle of formula on the wooden coffee table on top of a coaster. "Do people stay here often?"

"No. You're the first."

She would feel special if she hadn't picked up on a note of sadness in his voice. Figuring it was another off-limits subject, she picked up her baby and then settled into the deep couch adjacent to the fireplace.

Cash excused himself before bringing back her suitcase and taking it into the bedroom. He fished out his cell from his front pocket and frowned when he got a good look at the screen. It took a few seconds to scroll through all the messages he'd received in the last hour. Drawing his brows together, he shook his head before looking at her. When he did, he was distracted and she imagined there was more bad news about his father. Her heart went out to him. Cash O'Connor seemed like a decent man. One who didn't deserve what was happening.

"What's your cell number?" he asked.

She rattled off the digits. A second later, she heard a buzzing noise coming from her purse.

"Don't worry about it. I'm calling so you'll have my number in case you need anything." His buzzed again. He issued a sharp sigh after checking the screen and walking toward the door. "There's a spare set of keys hanging on a hook on the kitchen cabinet next to the garage door and a car should you need to use one. I texted you Stacy's number in case I'm not around or not getting cell coverage. It's spotty here on the ranch and especially in remote areas." He stopped short of crossing the threshold but his hand was on the knob. "I'll lock this on my way out. Not because it needs to be locked, but because it'll make you feel safer. I'll be back as soon as I can."

Renee smiled. It had been a very long time since anyone had had her back. Before she could thank Cash again, he darted out the door. The snick of the lock, as promised, allowed her to finally exhale.

THE FIRST LIGHT was rising against the night sky. Normally, Cash would stop long enough to appreciate the multicolored canopy that contained a mix of the most beautiful orange and blue hues. Texas had always felt like home and always had been. And yet there was something extra special about the land at KBR, something that fed Cash's soul.

Today, all he could think about was Pops.

Walking into the kitchen of the main house, Stacy made a beeline for him and nodded toward the back door. Cash turned and stepped onto the screened-in porch. He folded his arms across his chest as she joined him.

"Where is everyone?"

"I'm sorry, Cash." Those words dropped a lead anchor of dread in the pit of his stomach. "I thought it would be better to talk to you out here rather than have your mother be forced to rehash the details again."

"Has Pops turned up?" Even though Cash had a solid two inches of height on Finn O'Connor, the man would always stand eight feet tall in Cash's eyes. Not only was he a great father and husband, he was a great man. The thought of anything happening to Pops tightened the screws in his chest.

"Yes." Stacy studied the rug like her next words might be found there. When she looked back up at him, he could see water gathering in her eyes. Instead of speaking, she shook her head.

Cash knew exactly what she meant and yet his brain couldn't fathom anything happening to a strong man like Finn O'Connor. Since Stacy looked ready to crumble, Cash brought the older woman who'd been like an aunt to him into a hug. Sobs wracked her shoulders as disbelief cloaked Cash. There wasn't a world where it made sense his buck-strong and healthy sixty-eight-year-old father was suddenly gone.

Stacy pulled back and wiped her eyes, apologizing profusely.

"It's okay. You've been just as much a part of this family for the past thirty years as I have." His words seemed to strike a chord with Stacy. She managed a weak smile through her tears.

"I've been trying to hold it together for your mother. I didn't mean to unleash on you." Dark circles cradled her eyes, outlining her stress, and her rounded shoulders seemed even heavier now.

"You're doing all right." He was still trying to wrap his mind around the fact his father might be gone. He'd seen the same look of shock and disbelief more times than he could count on victims' faces. The brain seemed set on a delayed timer when it came to unfathomable news. Cash probably had that same look on his face now. He wanted to go inside to get more details, figure out how this could've happened and be a comfort to his mother. Stacy had been part of the family for as long as he could remember. There was no way he'd abandon her.

She twisted her fingers together. "It's all happening so fast. I mean, we knew he was sick but we just thought he'd magically pull through somehow. You know your father. The man was strong as an ox."

"Who knew he was sick?" Cash had been told about a couple of recent doctor's appointments. There'd been no serious illness news.

Stacy brought a hand up to cover her mouth. "I'm sorry. Your mother asked me not to say anything to any of the boys about his diagnosis."

Cash must've given her quite the look because she quickly added, "Aortic aneurysm."

"What is that exactly?"

"It's a bulge in a blood vessel that carries blood away from his heart. The doctors measured it and it fell within the guidelines. He was supposed to go back soon and have it rechecked." She shook her head and her voice was weary. "It must've grown faster than expected and ruptured. He collapsed on the property and Slim found him near Bridal Pass."

Slim Jenkins was ranch foreman. Cash bit his tongue. This shouldn't be the first time he was hearing about an issue with his father's health, but it wasn't Stacy's call to make. Pops would want to keep this information under the radar. Even though his children were all adults, he'd see the need to protect everyone. It was surprising that Pops had gone to the doctor in the first place. "Where's my mother?"

"She's inside in her bedroom." More tears spilled down Stacy's cheeks.

"And Pops?"

"An ambulance transported him…" A few more sobs wracked her as she tried to finish her sentence. She apologized again even though it was wholly unnecessary. There wasn't much Cash or his brothers wouldn't do for their family friend and ranch manager.

Reality started to sink in as Cash heard more details about his father's condition. His brain still rejected the fact that Finn O'Connor was anything but alive. Cash needed to see the rest of his family and yet his boots were rooted to the floor. He swiped a hand across his face, realized it had been a few days since he'd shaved. "Who's here?"

Stacy seemed to know exactly what he referred to when she started rattling off a few of his brothers' names. "Colton left with the ambulance and I haven't been able to reach Garrett."

"No surprises there." As sheriff, Colton would see it as his job to accompany the body and ensure there'd been no foul play. Garrett had a convenient habit of letting his phone run out of battery. He liked to disappear with no explanation, leaving their mother to worry. He'd always needed more space than the others. Between marriages, separations and divorces, the

O'Connor men had been preoccupied lately. "How long did Pops know about his medical condition?"

"Since last year," she admitted.

"And no one told us?"

"He said it wasn't a big enough deal to worry the family over. Your mom fussed at him, told him the boys deserved to know what was going on. He wasn't having it. He told her that he'd speak up when there was something worth talking about." She blew out a breath. "I don't have to remind you how stubborn your father could be."

Tightness built in Cash's chest. "It's a wonder she got him to go to the doctor in the first place."

"Her cholesterol numbers were running up and she was afraid his were doing the same. He didn't go willingly but he did go." Stacy's chin quivered. Cash's heart was breaking because in all the years he'd known her this was the first he'd seen her cry.

"Sounds about right." Cash grinned.

"Your father had no patience for anything that took him off his land or away from his family for longer than thirty minutes." Pops lived for the family ranch and the legacy the family had built over four generations. "Which shows how much more stubborn your mother is."

Margaret Ann O'Connor had a quiet strength, grace and dignity rarely seen. "She rarely takes no for an answer." And rarely had to speak above a whisper to get her way with Pops. The man was head over heels for his wife even to this day.

Was, Cash had to remind himself. That one word nearly gutted him. Finn O'Connor gone?

"I better let you go inside now. Thank you for giving me a few minutes, Cash. It means a lot."

"Any time you need to talk, I'm here." The look of appreciation she shot him was better than any verbal recognition. Actions always spoke the loudest.

With Stacy on better emotional footing, it was time to steel his resolve and face the rest of his family.

Chapter Five

When Cash walked into his mother's bedroom, the air changed. Palpable grief hit him like a surprise thunderstorm, hard and sudden. His mother was seated in her favorite reading chair by the window overlooking the expansive meadow on the east side of the family home. Three of his brothers stood nearby. No one seemed sure what to say in times of grief.

Blake spotted Cash first. His brother broke up the trio by making a beeline toward Cash. He couldn't help but notice the dark circles under Blake's eyes from worry and shock.

"Is it true?" Cash knew it was and yet part of him held out hope Stacy had bad information. She would never intentionally lie. The part of Cash's brain that couldn't accept the reality of his father's death took momentary control.

"Yes." Blake could be counted on to keep a cool head. Being second born and only eighteen months younger than Cash, the two had grown up best friends.

"Were there any signs of foul play?" Cash couldn't think of a soul who'd want to hurt Finn O'Connor. Years of experience had taught him that everyone had enemies whether they knew them or not.

"No." Blake shook his head for emphasis. This whole scene was confirmation of news he didn't want to be true. "Pops had a medical condition."

"Stacy filled me in. I just didn't want to believe it." Cash's words were met with a nod as brothers Riggs and Dawson joined the conversation. Cash glanced at his mother who sat with a rigid back, clutching a handkerchief and staring outside. She was the kind of mother who would think she needed to be strong for her kids, forget the fact she had six grown men for children now.

This wasn't the first time he'd seen her at that exact window with a similar look on her face, holding on to a handkerchief as though her life depended on it. Later, he'd learned why. A cavern opened in Cash's chest, the pain felt so palpable that it threatened to drag him under. Margaret O'Connor had always been there for him and he wanted to do the same for her. Although, he doubted she'd want to lean on one of her children.

"Before twenty minutes ago, I had no idea about Pops's condition," Riggs said. He was the tallest O'Connor by a quarter of an inch and normally liked to remind everyone when all the brothers were together. This time, he wore his sadness in the heavy lines bracketing his mouth and deep slashes across his forehead.

"Same," Blake said as the others agreed. The air in the room felt heavy.

Slim held the position of ranch foreman after working his way up from cleaning out stables. He'd become as trusted as Stacy, and as integral to running the family business. Cash realized how little he knew about the family business. Few of the O'Connor men had gone into ranching, only Garrett and Riggs. Pops had made no secret of the fact he wanted his sons to take over the family empire one day. With careers ranging from law enforcement to rancher, Garrett and Riggs were the only sons who'd followed in the family business. To prove a point, and basically be his stubborn self, Garrett had gone to work for a rival ranch.

"What was he doing over there alone?" Bridal Pass was a spot where folks called in favors from the O'Connors just to have the opportunity to take pictures against the beautiful backdrop of Texas's rolling hills. A few of the requests came from parents wanting to take their son or daughter's high-school-graduation pictures but most often a bridal party wanted to take wedding photos there, earning the place its nickname. Springtime was especially beautiful with bluebonnets for acres, making it the perfect location for photos. "He'd been checking fences, working right up until he collapsed."

There was a small measure of comfort knowing Pops went exactly the way he would have wanted to: working on his beloved ranch. "No one called a family meeting last year when he and Mother found out about his condition."

"We didn't think it would get worse so suddenly." His mother's attempt at bravery as she lifted her chin and pushed to standing lodged a rock in his chest. Breathing hurt while he had to fight every instinct that he had to march toward her and offer an arm. The only reason he didn't was because he knew in his heart she wouldn't want it.

"The doctors wanted to keep an eye on him." She shrugged. "I guess on some level we knew this was a possibility. He was overdue for his appointment. I should've insisted he take the time to go."

"This didn't happen because of something you did or didn't do." Cash beat his brothers to the punch. Any one of them would say the same thing. Their nods confirmed it. With him being eldest, the others usually showed him the respect of letting him speak first. Everyone except for Garrett. He challenged Cash and anyone else in authority for his own amusement.

Her weary steel-gray eyes pierced right through Cash. "You know how he gets this time of year."

Spring was the busiest time on a cattle ranch, with calving season. "Yes, ma'am."

"He seemed fine this morning." She paused. "But then your father wasn't the complaining type."

"No, ma'am." Cash spoke on behalf of his brothers.

A wistful smile upturned the corners of her lips and a little of the spark normally found in her eyes returned. "He was a mule when it came to doing anything he didn't want to do."

"Truer words have never been spoken, ma'am," Cash agreed and it seemed like everyone exhaled at the same time.

"He wouldn't want us to make a fuss about him," she quickly added, wagging a finger.

"No, he would not." Finn O'Connor was the most down-to-earth man. The term *salt-of-the-earth type* was tossed around a lot when people spoke of him even though he shied away from praise. His standards set the bar high. The man wore jeans and a button-down shirt no matter how hot it got outside. In Texas, that meant triple-digit summers. He always spoke about his wife, their mother, with the utmost love and respect. And, maybe more importantly, treated her that way.

"I miss him already." Mother wiped away a tear. "There'll be another huge hole in our lives now." The first she referred to was, of course, Cash's sister. The similarities between her kidnapping and Abby's near abduction brought an icy chill racing down Cash's back. Any time he came across a case involving a baby around the same age as his sister, he thought of her.

The hours-old kidnapping attempt hit a little too close to home. With literally decades between the crimes, the likelihood that the cases were related was next to none. Considering his mother was about to bury her husband, Cash didn't want to add to her sadness by dredging up old memories of Caroline. Their parents had launched several investigations over the years to find Cash's sister, none of which bore fruit. They'd been honest with their sons about what they were doing and why. Mother had brought out a small birthday cake every July 28 after supper for Caroline's birthday. The cake represented a mother's prayer that her child was alive and being well cared for. It was accompanied by a quick prayer and a few precious shared memories.

For Abby's attempted kidnapping, the perp couldn't possibly be the same person. Caroline's kidnapping happened more than thirty years ago. If the perp had been in his twenties back then, he would be in his fifties now. Not impossible but definitely not likely. There hadn't been another kidnapping or attempt involving a six-month-old girl in town for three decades.

Cash should know. He and his brothers who worked in law enforcement had searched cold cases for similar crimes. Deep down, he wanted to bring closure to his family.

Margaret O'Connor had enough to deal with at present.

"Has anyone been able to reach your brother?" Everyone knew who their mother was talking about. Garrett. The man changed cell phone numbers more often than some people changed shirts, or so it seemed.

"Not that I know of." Cash fished his cell out of his pocket and held it up. "Does anyone have his latest number?"

"I don't think so," Riggs said.

Being an investigator, it shouldn't be this difficult to keep tabs on his own brother. And yet, Garrett knew a thing or two about not being found when it suited him. It wasn't unlike him to disappear for weeks or months on end. Being busy with his own life, Cash didn't think much of it. It was always just Garrett's way. He'd show eventually. No one had really needed to find him until now. Outsider or not, Garrett needed to know about their father. "I'll make a few calls. See if I can come up with something."

Their mother smiled. "In the meantime, how about I put on a pot of fresh brew?"

From the looks of his brothers, everyone needed a drink a helluva lot stronger than coffee. That cold beer sounded better and better to Cash. He wiped a hand across the stubble on his face, figuring coffee was the most appropriate option at this hour despite being up most of the night.

"I'll take a cup." Riggs was the first to speak up. The others nodded. "I can make a pot if—"

"I'll do it." Their mother was petite and thin with a soft voice, but also stubborn. She was always well put together, kind and a gentle encourager. Still beautiful inside and out. She also had a full head of hair, something she joked that her sons would thank her for later in life since it was rumored boys inherited the bald gene from the mother's side.

Their mother loved her library and spent many a night there long after her usual bedtime reading one of her novels.

A few of his brothers exchanged glances as their mother walked out of the room. Margaret Ann O'Connor did a lot of things. However, making coffee wasn't one of them.

No matter what else was going on, she woke at four o'clock on the dot six days a week to be with their father to eat breakfast with him before he headed out for the day. No one would ever accuse her of being a morning person and yet she managed to smile through her yawns. A cup of coffee later, and she'd spend mornings working in their home office. Pops used to say that she was a whiz with numbers. A good day to Pops meant being on the land with the animals, working side by side with his foreman and ranch hands.

Cash excused himself to make a couple of calls so he could try to track down their missing brother. Garrett came off like he didn't care, but that couldn't be true. It seemed like he'd been born with a chip on his shoulder and Cash couldn't figure out why for the life of him.

Last Cash heard, his brother worked on another ranch as a hand. The guy was heir to one of the biggest cattle fortunes in the state of Texas and he worked for little better than minimum wage, a roof over his head and three square meals a day. There couldn't be a better way to thumb his nose at his upbringing or his family.

Owning mineral rights on the family land had made the family beyond wealthy and Pops wasn't afraid to share the wealth with the men who worked for him. Speaking of whom, Cash needed to see who planned to tell the hands what was going on. The news should come from one of Finn's sons.

Garrett was the first priority. Cash used his phone to look up the website of his brother's last known employer. He found it easily enough and then located contact information. This situation necessitated a call rather than an impersonal text. He entered the number and hit the call button.

"Thank you for calling Bullman Ranch." The female voice was perky. The young person sounded barely out of high school. She had a drawl to her voice that was decidedly country.

"My name is Cash O'Connor. I'm looking for my brother, Garrett. Last I heard, he worked at your ranch." He didn't see the need to say her parents' ranch, that was obvious. He also decided against using his law-enforcement title. It might scare her into thinking Garrett was in some kind of legal trouble.

"Oh, sorry. He took off weeks ago. No notice. He just up and left after an argument with his foreman." She sounded genuinely sad to deliver the news.

"Any idea where he might have gone?" Cash could've figured as much. It sounded like something Garrett would do.

"No, sir. My dad wants me to tell anyone who asks about him not to hire him and that if Garrett wants to get paid he needs to see my dad for a check. My dad didn't okay the electronic deposit like usual."

"I'll pass along the message next time I see him."

"That would be awesome."

Cash thanked her and ended the call.

HOURS HAD PASSED since Cash had left and Renee realized Abby's pacifier must've fallen out of her mouth either back at home or in his vehicle. It was midafternoon and she couldn't find the darn thing anywhere near Abby. After walking around the guest cottage with a crying baby over her shoulder for close to half an hour, she needed to come up with a plan. Going back to the farmhouse wasn't an option until she knew who was behind the kidnapping attempt and the jerk was behind bars.

There wasn't much more terrifying than moving to a new place, not knowing a soul and having a baby to care for. All of which was trumped by the crime that had happened last night. Between work and Jamison's sick mother, Renee was beginning to realize how small her circle had become. People she'd believed to be friends at work started avoiding her once word got around that she was helping care for a terminal patient. No one was obvious about it. At least, not at first. Then the lunch invites had started to dwindle. The sadder and more miserable Renee became by staying in a relationship whose breakup was long overdue, the more often she declined invitations. She'd reasoned that no one wanted to be around a killjoy and nothing depressed a mood like her being honest about two major things in her life: the end of her relationship and his mother's condition.

Sadly, those two things quickly became her life. Waking up at five to go to the gym and get in a workout every morning had become her saving grace. Looking back, it was almost comical that Jamison had accused her of cheating on him with the spin class instructor. She should've realized he was just trying to throw her off his trail. But his jealous streak had only increased over the years. He'd become more and more possessive. He would've freaked out if he'd known what Darion had pulled at work.

Jamison dropped the cheating subject real fast

when she'd invited him to start coming to class with her.

Abby almost quieted as Renee gently bounced her up and down. Just when Renee was ready to declare victory, the little girl pulled in a deep breath and belted out the most heart-wrenching cry. "I'm sorry, Abby. I promise I'll get better at this. I'll figure out what you want."

Renee patted the little girl's back. She wondered if she should sit around and wait for Cash to show back up. After a few more laps around the cottage, desperation was mounting. Renee had to do something besides pace and pat her daughter's back. Abby was fed and her diaper was clean. Renee needed that pacifier.

Didn't Cash mention there was a set of keys to a vehicle outside?

Without hesitation, Renee moved to the key that was hanging on a hook in the kitchen next to the garage door. She put her daughter in her carrier and buckled it into the car. Renee and daughter were on the paved road toward the exit inside of five minutes.

Using the navigation system on her phone, she programmed in the nearest grocery store, figuring it would have a pacifier, and then from memory made it to the security gate leading off the property. At least the sun was going strong on a cloudless spring day. Abby settled down by the time Renee turned onto the main road into town. She'd be lost without GPS and her phone. Cash had mentioned there were spots on the ranch with no service. The thought made her want to shudder.

There were only a few vehicles on the road for the longest time. The car ride had soothed Abby back to sleep. Renee reluctantly pulled into the parking lot of the Green Grocers and found a space. A dozen vehicles dotted the parking lot. It wasn't full by Dallas standards but she had a sneaking suspicion it might be busy for the small town of Katy Gulch. And it was good she was getting out and learning the area.

Busy unbuckling her daughter's carrier that doubled as a car seat, Renee barely noticed when a car pulled up near hers and parked. Out of the corner of her eye, she did see another block hers in. Palming her keys and placing one in between her first and second finger, she fisted her right hand. Shoulders back, she set the car seat in the back and figured she could slam her car door into anyone who got close. With the jagged side of the key ready, she scanned the area. Pressing the panic alarm on the key fob could scare the baby.

Heart in her throat, she steeled her breath as the driver of the car near hers exited his vehicle. Glancing around, she cursed the fact it seemed like everyone was inside the store. Of course, the perps would plan it that way, she reasoned.

In a split second, three men were coming at her. All of the men wore baggy clothes, hoodies and sunglasses. It was impossible to get a look at their faces, considering they'd wrapped scarves around them.

Renee's pulse jackhammered. This couldn't be happening. Who would want to take Abby? Because Renee was certain they came for the baby, just like last night. No place felt safe. Renee knew one thing was certain, no one was taking Abby away from her.

Despite the three-to-one odds, Renee had no intention of handing over her daughter. "I don't know what you want but you need to leave." The words came out shakier than she'd hoped.

One of the guys shook his head. She blocked the carrier with her body and the door. As two of the men came directly at her, another one slipped out of sight. She realized a little too late that he'd come around to the passenger side. He opened the door. It would be so easy for him to slip the carrier out.

Renee needed to draw attention if she was to have any hope these men would scatter. Fighting three off at one time wouldn't end well. At the top of her lungs, she screamed, "Fire."

It was a trick she'd learned a long time ago

from a neighbor who'd been a fireman. He'd taught her never to yell for help, always fire. People rushed toward a fire. Help, they might ignore.

"Fire." She yelled with so much force that she startled the baby. She vowed not to let these jerks take off with Abby. Desperation mounted as one of the men got close enough for her to take a swipe at him. He ducked and pinned her using the door as leverage.

Again, she yelled the word she'd been taught. With the door trapping her against the vehicle, she reached back to grab the handle of the carrier. Pain shot through her but a shot of adrenaline kicked in. The guy wasn't taking her baby. The two struggled for control of the carrier as she screamed over and over again.

Just when she thought she might be holding her ground, her fingers were being peeled off the handle. A wave of panic shot through her. Panic and more anger as she struggled for purchase.

One of the guys sneered at her as he pressed his body against the door, keeping her from moving or fighting back. Her last finger slipped from the carrier when she heard the sirens. Movement hurt, but she managed to use her elbow as a wedge to shove the door. The guy blew out a breath and dug his shoes into the concrete.

"Hey!" A man's voice shouted from the direction of the store. Help was on the way. Was it going to be too late?

Chapter Six

In a matter of seconds, sirens filled the air and a few men came running. A car squealed its tires, roaring into the parking lot. Suddenly the pressure from the door was gone and Abby's cries were right behind Renee.

Abby. Her daughter was in the back seat as the three men jumped in their respective vehicles and peeled out of the parking lot in the opposite direction. All Renee wanted to do was hold her baby. She climbed in the back seat as an older gentleman darted toward her.

"Are you okay, miss?" The middle-aged man with a slight build and jean jacket stopped at her vehicle.

"Yes, thank you." She would be when she got Abby out of that car seat. Everything had happened so fast that she didn't get a good look at the vehicles. "Did anyone get a picture of those creeps or their vehicles?"

"I really don't know. I can ask." Looking up,

she saw that he wore an apron that read Green Grocers.

Before she could say anything else, a car rushed into the spot next to hers. The face of the driver sent another shock wave rippling through her. Cash O'Connor. He tore out of the driver's seat.

"Everybody take a deep breath and an even bigger step away from the vehicle." His voice poured over her, soothing her fried nerves.

The small crowd complied as the man wearing the apron gave a quick explanation of what he'd witnessed.

"Hold tight. I'm going to get you and Abby out of here." Those words were the best thing she'd heard all day. She was grateful that Cash hadn't asked how she was doing. Now that he was there and the immediate threat had passed, her hands started shaking.

"I was trying to buy a pacifier." The words sounded a little hollow, even to her.

"It's okay. You're all right. Abby's good." There was something so calm about Cash as he stood there, taking statements and handling the nervous crowd. Except when he looked at her, she caught a storm brewing behind his steel gaze. "I'm taking you home. Colton can meet us there to take your statement."

Cash offered a hand and she took it. He

helped her out of the back seat. One look at her iron grip on the car seat handle and he seemed to think better of asking if she wanted him to carry the baby. He walked her over to his SUV where she climbed in the back with the baby. Renee secured the buckle and scooted so close to the carrier that it was practically on her lap. He locked up the other vehicle before claiming the driver's seat.

"Tell me everything that just happened." He started the ignition and reversed out of the lot. She couldn't wait to put this whole experience in the rearview. Somehow, this seemed like the beginning of a nightmare.

She briefed him on the events and tried to calm her racing heart in the process as he made his way back toward his family's ranch. "It was three to one and I thought they had her for a minute there. Thank you for showing when you did."

"Security alerted me to the fact that you left. I heard the call come in." There was a weariness to his voice that wasn't there before.

"You left to check on your father. Did they find him all right?"

"He was found." The heaviness in those three words told her the news wasn't good.

"I'm so sorry. I mean it, Cash." Words seemed

hollow compared to what he must be feeling right now.

"Thank you. It means a lot." He nodded and she caught his gaze through the rearview. A powerful jolt rocketed through her body the minute their eyes locked. The force was so strong, her cheeks flamed and she diverted her gaze to Abby.

The attraction between them was so powerful, Renee straightened her daughter's pajamas to give her something else to focus on besides the current rippling through the vehicle.

Trying to apply logic to an out-of-control emotional situation made her think the strong pull to Cash O'Connor had to do with how broken he seemed. She could relate on such a deep level to the loss she'd glimpsed in him during those few seconds of eye contact. Hers was so much more than a relationship gone sour. Granted, that didn't help matters.

The rest of the ride was spent in companionable silence. Once they were back on O'Connor property, Cash stopped at the turnoff to the guesthouse.

"I need to check on my family and I won't be able to think straight if I'm wondering if the two of you are okay."

"I'm sorry about—"

"That came out wrong." He put his hand on

the seat in front of her and twisted around to face her. "I care about what happens to the two of you. Leaving you alone to fend for yourself in a stranger's house was a jerk move on my part. I apologize for putting you in a bad position. I'd like to make it up to you, if you'll allow it. Right now, though, I need to get back to my family. I need to know what you want me to do. I can take you back to the cottage or to the main house with me."

The thought of being alone again didn't sit well with Renee. She had no doubt she'd get her bearings as a mother, but a lot had been thrown at her considering she couldn't exactly go home. "The main house is fine with me, Cash. I appreciate everything you're doing for us. I don't want to take advantage of your hospitality, though."

He started to argue but she put a hand up to stop him.

"I'm serious. If you need to do your job, I don't want to be in the way."

"You couldn't be," was all he said. "And for the record, it's not putting me out to help you and your daughter. I'm a selfish jerk because I'll admit that it feels good to impact someone else's life. It's the whole reason I got into law enforcement in the first place. As cliché as it sounds, I wanted to put bad people behind bars and help deserving people."

When he put it like that, her shoulders deflated a little because a growing part of her wanted to be special in his eyes. The reminder that he was a lawman who was doing his job was just what she needed to hear in order to save her from some potential embarrassment later. To Renee, there was nothing ordinary about her feelings toward Cash. "There's a reason clichés are what they are. They always contain a grain of truth."

CASH PARKED HIS vehicle in the small lot at the main house. Bringing a victim into his family's home was a little unorthodox. The way he saw it, there was no other choice. He couldn't rightly leave Renee alone. She was still new at being a mother. Add to the fact that she'd moved to a new town and on her first night there had become a crime statistic. This wasn't the welcome most folks received in Katy Gulch. Considering there'd been very little crime in town, residents might see her presence as an omen. People could be superstitious. He saw it as his job to make certain she and Abby were safe. He told himself the reason he cared so much was because of the lost look in her eyes and the fire that followed. A crime might have occurred, but she seemed determined not to be a victim.

Based on their conversations so far, she was intelligent. Her beauty was a given. Fiery red hair and blue eyes on a heart-shaped face made for one seriously beautiful package. She had legs that went on for days and which most runners would envy. Her creamy skin and the flush to her cheeks added to her beauty. Looks alone had never been the biggest draw for Cash. Going on a date with someone who was pretty on the outside and empty on the inside was a lot like expecting cake and getting cornbread instead. He'd gone on a handful of dates based on physical attraction alone. Most could be rated by how many times he sneaked a peek at his watch. Those were generally sixes, meaning he checked his watch six times in a two-hour span.

He'd gotten good at predicting his number within ten minutes of a date. He suspected a date with Renee would net a zero. And, since the attraction to her was inappropriate considering she was his witness, he'd stop himself right there.

"Who would come back for her?" Renee asked as she unbuckled her daughter from her carrier and then held the little girl against her chest. The fire had returned to her eyes, which was a helluva lot better than the fear he'd seen there back in the grocery lot.

"There's a long list of people I'd like to talk to before I can answer that question." The rock stirred underneath his breastbone.

"Starting where?"

"With your lawyer. I'll need to coordinate the investigation with my brother, considering he's the sheriff. But I'd like to interview everyone involved in the adoption process."

"I thought you'd start with my ex," she admitted.

"He's on the list, too. And so is the contractor from work. As is anyone else you've come into contact with who might've had a bone to pick with you. Including your ex's new girlfriend."

Renee gasped. She held on to her daughter protectively. It would be hard to imagine anyone could pry the little girl from her hands. Cash had never thought of himself as a family man. He thought that ship had sailed a long time ago, after his last broken heart.

"I hadn't thought of her before. What reason would she have to want to take my child away from me?"

"A few come to mind. She might've lost her baby. She could've lied about being pregnant in the first place. He might have left her because he was still in love with you."

She blew out a breath. "I know he still has feelings for me. He's made that clear on more than one occasion. But I've been very honest with him. I've moved on and he should, too."

"The man's a fool," came out low and under his breath. Even the most intelligent person could make a bad decision when it came to someone they were attracted to. Renee had said she'd been with her ex for seven years, which meant she would've been in her early twenties when they'd met. "I'll put my head together with my brother. He'll be able to offer more perspective on the case."

Cash had to admit his growing feelings for the mother and child would impact his judgment. As an investigator, he needed to maintain objectivity in a case. Jamison King was an idiot for losing Renee.

He quirked a smile. So much for being objective.

More immediately, he needed to prepare Renee for what she was about to walk into at his family's home.

"As a warning, my family can be overwhelming to someone not used to us. Normally, we're a loud and caring bunch. The caring part is still true but finding out about my father has put the mood in the house at a somber level."

"It's to be expected under the circumstances."

She practically pinned him with her stare. "Again, I'm so sorry for your loss."

"Your kindness is appreciated when it comes to my family." The O'Connors might not be perfect but their love for each other ran deep. No matter how big a mistake any of them made in life, the others rallied. Garrett included, despite his noticeable absence in recent years.

"Are you sure it's a good idea for me to be here while your family is going through so much?"

He tilted his head to one side. "You wouldn't be here if I didn't think it was a good idea."

"Fair enough."

"The timing isn't ideal but then there's never a good time to lose someone you love."

The look she gave him said she completely understood the sentiment. Cash tried to tell himself that he wanted to get to know more about Renee because of the investigation. A voice in the back of his mind called him out on the lie. There was something magnetic about the beautiful redhead, that clap of thunder he hadn't felt in far too long.

"Ready?" he asked.

She nodded.

He placed his hand on her elbow as he led her inside the main house. Her eyes widened as she stepped into the foyer of the two-story mansion his parents had called home for longer than Cash was alive.

"Wow," she muttered and he realized how impressive the place could be. He'd honestly gotten so used to it he'd forgotten how grand it could be. Big homes and expensive cars had never really impressed him much. His family was as down-to-earth as they came.

"My grandfather had this home built. My parents moved in to help take care of him when he became sick and he asked them to stay on. Mother always said she never really needed a place this big but it seemed important to her father-in-law. He was a kind man and she saw no reason to offend him. She'd had the downstairs renovated to her taste once they inherited the home, careful to keep important original details."

"Like?"

"A library with handcrafted bookshelves. You rarely ever see those built in homes now."

"That's so true. I love modern plumbing, don't get me wrong, but I've never even thought about having a full-fledged library in my home." There was so much awe in Renee's voice it was impossible not to let it affect him a little bit.

"Mother is old-school. I can't remember a time when she turned on a TV. We had 'em. Well, one. It's in the game room where we spent plenty of Sunday afternoons shooting pool, throwing darts and watching football when it was in season and chores were done."

"Sounds pretty great to me." She nodded and smiled, a first break in the tension that had been blanketing her. Football and Texans generally went hand in hand. "And it seems like I could learn quite a few parenting pointers from your mother. Your parents have obviously done a wonderful job with their boys."

"We had a sister," he admitted. He should probably prep her for the reaction his mother might have to a six-month-old girl being in the house. "Remember the sister I mentioned? She was kidnapped when she was little." He left it at that for the time being.

"Oh?" Shocked blue eyes blinked at him.

"My mother is strong, but I'm not sure she ever completely recovered from losing her daughter." Because he felt the need to change the subject before she asked too many questions, he added, "I hope you're not allergic to animals. We have quite a few critters running around the property."

"Are you kidding? I love animals." Her face brightened in the way only an animal lover's would. She glanced around, hugging Abby tight to her chest.

"Do you want something to drink first?" It

might be almost evening but he could do with another coffee. When security had called to alert him to the fact that Renee had left the property he'd acted on impulse, jumping into a vehicle and taking off toward town. He'd guessed she wouldn't go back to her house. It was an assumption that had paid off. He didn't want to think what might've happened to Abby if he hadn't shown up when he did.

Timing wasn't always this good to him. He'd take it where he could.

"Coffee sounds good. I didn't get much in the way of sleep last night." She glanced at the sleeping angel now. "She started crying right after you left and nothing I did helped. You seem to have some kind of magic with her."

He didn't point out the fact she'd probably worn herself out crying earlier. "Give it a little time. You're doing better than you probably think."

"What makes you so sure?"

"I know how much my brother second-guessed himself when it came to his twins, especially in those first few months."

"I can barely manage with one. How on earth does he do this with two?"

"He had his rough patches in the early days but he's in a good rhythm now." Cash led her into the kitchen and then fixed two cups of coffee, surprised that no one was hanging around. His mother had most likely retreated to her library with her friend and Stacy. He was pretty sure he'd seen Gayle's car still parked out front. His brothers were probably in the barn, having a conversation with Slim and the others. "I'm afraid self-doubt seems to come with the territory for new parents." He set a cup in front of her on the massive butcher-block island. "It's easy to see how much you care about doing right by her. No one who cares that much could possibly fail."

She took a seat on one of the barstools and repositioned the baby, cradling her with one arm. "Thank you for finding her pacifier in your car. And I sure hope you're right. I've always wanted to be a mother. Life wasn't exactly ideal for a long time so I didn't think much about it but then lately it's like everything in my life snapped into place and I just knew the timing was right. For her. For a change. For a new life."

"Can't say that I have personal experience with an epiphany like that one, but I have always felt like I was supposed to be in law enforcement from as early as I can remember." He paused long enough to take a sip. "Which brings me to my next action. Calling in my brother."

"Are you sure that's a good idea with what

your family is going through?" she asked pensively.

"Work is good for grief and there's a kidnapper on the loose in Katy Gulch." He stopped short of saying words like *kidnapping ring*. "Besides, we'll be grieving my father for a long time to come." Cash could scarcely contemplate the hole their father's death was going to leave in the family. If sadness got hold of Cash, it might not let him go. So, he decided it was best to deal with his emotions in doses rather than try to take it all in at once. It would swallow him up otherwise.

"As long as you're sure I won't be in the way." Those big blue eyes searched his for confirmation.

Cash was one hundred percent in trouble when it came to the little family sitting in his mother's kitchen. Nothing was going to happen to either of them on his watch. It was a promise he knew he couldn't guarantee no matter how much his heart wanted to.

The buzz of his cell phone indicated a text had come in. Cash glanced at the screen and then looked up. "Colton is parking right now."

Chapter Seven

Colton walked into the kitchen where Cash greeted him. The two embraced in a bear hug that nearly melted Renee's heart. Having grown up an only child, she had learned early on in life to depend on herself.

"Renee, I'd like you to meet my brother Colton O'Connor, the sheriff." Cash practically beamed with pride when he introduced his brother.

Colton extended his hand. Renee accepted the offering with a solid shake.

"I'm really sorry about your father." She meant those words. Mr. O'Connor must have been a wonderful father and man to have raised such amazing sons. It was easy to see both Cash and Colton were honest, respectful and kind men.

"Thank you for your kindness. We can't begin to fill the void our father leaves behind." Colton nodded his appreciation.

"He gave us a lot to live up to, that's for sure," Cash added. The warmth Renee witnessed between the brothers drew out a surprise longing to be part of a big family. She had always wanted to be a mother. But she figured hers would be a *one-and-done* situation. The sudden picture of big family holidays with three or four kids running around sent warmth shooting through her. She chalked the sentiment up to overwrought nerves and the biology class that had taught her about ingrained primal needs when it came to protection. A large close-knit family would offer more defense during a dangerous time.

Having a baby made her feel more vulnerable than she'd expected. Renee was slowly realizing just how much motherhood would change her. Hearing Cash review details as he brought his brother up to speed made her realize she needed to add security measures if she ever wanted to sleep at night after this ordeal. Having a complete stranger come inside her home without permission made her feel violated and angry.

"It's too early to rule anything out but I'm not as worried about the general population of town being at risk now that I've been caught up." Colton's lips formed a thin line. "On the surface, this crime appears to be targeted at Ms. Smith and her daughter."

"Please, call me Renee." She'd suspected as much. However, hearing those words caused her to hold Abby just a little bit closer.

Colton conceded her request with a small smile and a nod. She also noticed that his gaze moved from her back to his brother where it lingered a few seconds too long. In her mind, the attraction happening between her and Cash had been mostly on her side until then. Watching his brother, she was thinking that maybe the feeling was mutual. No one had ever stirred her heart or made her stomach free-fall the way he did. As much as she wanted to run toward the feeling, it was best to leave well enough alone.

"Since this does appear to be a targeted crime," Colton continued, "I'd like to start interviewing those closest to the witness."

Cash nodded in agreement. It seemed both investigators were on the same track.

"We can interview suspects together, separately or split the list. However you want to get this done. You're the lead on this one." Cash rocked on his heels.

"Considering there have been two attempts in less than a day, it makes more sense to split the list so we can cover more ground, faster." Colton paused a few beats. "It might be a good idea for me to call and ask suspects to stop by my office so you can watch them give statements from behind the glass of the interview room. Hearing the statements might spark something and we'll hopefully get further." He made a good point. One that had his brother rocking his head in agreement one more time. Colton looked to Renee. "I'd like to start with your ex."

"Agreed," Cash stated. "With a family on the way, he shouldn't be a flight risk. Asking him to come and give a statement shouldn't raise any red flags. We're merely requesting that he make an appointment to stop by, which seems a lot less threatening than showing up at his home or job."

"Very true." Colton cocked his head to one side. "I don't like the lawyer on the adoption case. His name has come up far too often in questionable cases."

Renee gasped. "Does that mean my adoption could be illegal?" Fear gripped her, squeezing the air out of her lungs.

"It's too early to make any predictions in this case and I know he's had legal adoptions to his credit." Colton's reassurance fell short of comforting her.

"He's like oil," Cash said. He and his brother seemed to be on the same page when it came to Kipp McGee.

"Nothing sticks," Colton agreed.

"The unknown guy from the moving company tops my list, as well." Cash tapped his phone where he'd been keeping notes. "As does the contractor from her office, Darion."

Hearing the names of possible suspects—people who wanted to hurt her—sent a chill racing down her back. Discussing her life and people in it struck her as surreal. Then again, after being stagnant for so long, at least her life was moving forward again. This situation was awful and creepy but at least she was living again.

"Her ex's new girlfriend has my attention as well. Do you happen to know the name of her boss?" Colton asked Renee. "I want to be able to verify their whereabouts from an independent source. I also might need to call her during the day to ask her to come in."

"Yolanda Tran works for the same person Jamison does. The guy's name is Adam Sartre." She gently rocked Abby who was surprisingly still asleep. Bedtime wasn't that far off and Renee might pay dearly for letting her angel sleep this late in the day but she didn't want to disturb Abby.

"Do you work at the same place?" he asked.

"Yes, but different departments. They work in sales and I work behind the scenes keeping our company's website up-to-date with products. We sell tax software. The company name is TaxedUp."

"A quick call to their boss might help answer a few questions." Colton got up and poured a glass of water. "Considering the first attack happened in the middle of the night, no one with a nine-to-five office job would've been at work. So, we can't rule anyone out based on the timeline. However, today's attempt is a different story." He looked at Renee. "Can you provide a cell number to Adam Sartre?"

With her free hand, Renee fished her cell phone from her pocket and scrolled through the contacts. She stopped on Adam's number. "This is his number." She rattled it off.

Colton thanked her. "Let me give him a quick call and see if we can find out if they were at work during the second attempt."

He excused himself before walking back to the sink to refill his glass. "Good evening. Is this Mr. Sartre?"

He must've said it was because Colton continued after a beat. "My name is Sheriff Colton O'Connor and I'd like to ask a couple of questions about two of your employees if I could have a moment of your time." There was silence for a few beats. "Yes, sir. I'm calling about Jamison King and Yolanda Tran." There was another pause. "Did either one of them show up for work today?" Another pause. "Neither?"

Renee's heart dropped. As mad as she was at Jamison for everything he'd done during their relationship and especially the past year, the thought he could be involved with a kidnapping attempt on Abby nearly gutted her. Losing his mother had accelerated the changes in him. Could he actually be that cruel?

Hearing the lawyer that she'd used for the adoption was shady sent her mind in another direction. Was it possible Abby's birth parents wanted her back? Had Abby been taken from someone illegally? Granted, if that were true it seemed like the person would use regular channels to get their daughter back. The court system would be the first line of defense for Abby's parents if she'd been taken illegally. Plus, wouldn't there be an AMBER alert issued? Cell phones would have been blasted and her picture would be all over the news.

Unless whoever had given the baby up had changed his or her mind. The mother or father could have known Kipp McGee wasn't honest. He might even have paid them good money to stay quiet. The person might have followed him to Renee. In that case, Renee might have the upper hand legally. But then she could end up bankrupting herself fighting it out in court.

Her brain cramped thinking there might be some way she could lose her daughter.

Renee couldn't go there. Not even hypothetically. Her gaze searched Cash's for some kind of reassurance. It should be odd that a man she barely knew had become like a lifeline in a matter of hours. And yet, there was something different about Cash O'Connor that she couldn't quite put her finger on. No man before him made her feel comforted when her world was careening toward the wall. In all the years she'd been together with Jamison, she'd never once had a sense of belonging or of the world being right.

Again, she blamed biology. Cash was strong and intelligent. He wore a badge. The man was clearly capable of handling any situation that came his way. Having someone around who she could lean on for a change was foreign but nice. She could get used to being a team with someone like Cash.

The situation was temporary, a little voice in the back of her mind reminded her. After the investigation, he'd go back to his life and she'd go back to hers.

So, why did the thought make her sad?

They both lived in Katy Gulch. She planned to stick around. With a stubborn streak a mile long, she had no plans to repack her belongings and head back to Dallas. Security needed to be installed to make her environment safer. Katy Gulch was home now.

His brother ended the call and shot her a look of apology. "Neither Mr. King nor Ms. Tran made it in to work this morning. She wasn't feeling well so she called in sick. Mr. King told their boss she made a doctor's appointment and he wanted to be there since the pregnancy was progressing."

"Does that mean what I think it does? She is his alibi and vice versa?" Was that even allowed? Renee had no idea how the law worked or how a judge would view testimony from someone who had a vested interest in hiding the truth.

"I'm afraid so. I can have my assistant dig up information about her doctor, see if they made it to their appointment this morning." Colton drummed his fingers on the granite island as Cash's gaze intensified.

"It'll be interesting to hear what they have to say." Renee couldn't help but roll her eyes. Interesting wasn't exactly the word that usually came to mind when she thought of Jamison.

Cash grunted. "I definitely want to be behind the glass of the interview room to hear their excuses in person."

"I'm going to make some calls on my way

in to my office. See how fast we can get meetings set up for tomorrow. I want to move on this quickly before this perp has a chance to regroup and strike again." Colton's words sent another icy chill down Renee's spine. He turned to her. "You'll be in good hands with my brother here. As a US marshal, protecting a witness is one of the many things he does well. Don't hesitate to reach out to me if you remember anything that might help with the case."

"We'll head out soon." Cash's jaw tightened and it looked like he clenched his back teeth.

She thanked Colton again for everything he was doing for her and Abby. It surprised Renee that she wanted to be more to Cash than just a work assignment.

THE BABY HAD been fed and was happily sleeping. The little thing barely had any hair but she made up for it with the biggest brown eyes—eyes that melted hearts. Cash had been cycling through a few thoughts while Renee took care of the baby's immediate needs.

He had a dozen thoughts running through his mind. It was possible Jamison and Yolanda had something against Renee. Revenge? Why? What would they have to gain by taking her child? The thought occurred to him that something might've happened to Yolanda's pregnancy to make her lose her baby. Then Abby would be a replacement. Still, why? It didn't quite add up that the two of them would be in league against her. What would Yolanda have to gain? Jamison didn't seem to want a child. Or, maybe he didn't want a child with Renee, in which case the man was an idiot.

Renee was an intelligent, beautiful woman. Any man would be lucky to have her in his life. Jamison must be a real piece of work.

It was altogether possible that Jamison had realized that he'd made a mistake walking away from Renee. It was worth considering the position Yolanda would be in should Jamison declare he was still in love with his ex. But why try to kidnap the baby? Why not go after Renee directly? Taking Abby to hurt Renee was a roundabout way to punish her. Yolanda dropped a few notches down the suspect list.

Since this was a targeted crime and he and his brother had been focused on someone looking to punish Renee, it was worth considering the birth mother or father simply wanted their child back. Kipp McGee wasn't exactly known for dealing aboveboard.

A young mother or father who'd changed their mind had motive. It might even make more sense. The mover, in Cash's opinion, was a pawn if he was involved. He was a tool meant to accomplish a goal. He could also lead them to the real perp. Figuring out his identity could be the lead they needed to crack the case open. Cash couldn't count the number of times a case had exploded after a small piece of information lit a fire, creating a domino effect.

Then there was the contractor from Renee's job. The guy was a creep and most definitely out of line. Was he the criminal they were looking for?

Cash's thoughts circled back to Kipp McGee. That was the interview Cash most wanted to listen in on. When he got the green light to take Renee to his brother's office, he needed to have a conversation with Colton about the lawyer, who moved up the suspect list based on his reputation in the law enforcement community.

"Any word from your brother?" Renee had kept Abby within arm's reach since they'd arrived at his family's home. She must need a break by now but she seemed determine not to let the little girl out of her sight and he couldn't blame her. If the shoe was on the other foot and it was *his* daughter, he wouldn't let her out of his sight until he taught her basic self-defense moves.

"Nothing yet." He wondered if he could convince her to eat something or go to sleep. "Are you hungry?"

Renee shook her head. "Not really."

"I can't speak from personal experience, but my brother Colton swears the only time he got any rest was when his twins were asleep." Cash glanced at the carrier.

Renee blew out a frustrated-sounding breath. "I seriously doubt I'll ever close my eyes again after what happened. I've literally never been so shaken up in my life." She shook her head and pinched the bridge of her nose. "That must make me sound a little crazy."

"Not really. I saw how much having children changed my brother. I'm pretty sure crazy comes with the job." The fact that she laughed at his joke made his chest puff out a little bit more than he should probably allow. It was the first break in tension and she very much needed it. Being on alert that long and overstressed wasn't good for Renee. Cash had seen it countless times with witnesses in his protection.

"I'm beginning to see that now." Her smile didn't exactly reach her eyes, but he'd take it. It was progress. She was quick to add, "I still think it's the best job in the world."

He had no idea. No plans to figure it out, either. Cash had seen his brother go through falling in love, having kids. And then having his heart cut in half when his wife walked because law enforcement was too risky a job. It was true. Only a special kind of person could hang in there not knowing whether or not the love of their life would walk through the door at night. Many men and women couldn't handle their spouses putting their lives on the line on a daily basis.

Cash would argue figuring that out after getting married and birthing babies was ridiculous. Colton's wife had known the risks going in. His brother had been sheriff for the past five years. Vows meant something to an O'Connor. There was no backing out after going to the altar. And Cash was in no rush to jump feet first into that pool.

Renee was different. She beamed at the mention of Abby. "It suits you. Being a mother. Looks good on you."

Her cheeks flushed at the compliment and she was even more beautiful. His heart betrayed him again by clenching and making him wish he had more time to get to know Renee outside of his job.

"Thank you. I have a long way to go before I get a handle on parenting, so I'm surprised it looks good on me." She laughed. It was a small win, but he'd take it. Making Renee relax a little bit after what she'd been through made him feel good.

"You make it work." He smiled back at her. "Do you mind if I ask a personal question?"

"Go ahead. I have a feeling after all this is said and done you will end up knowing a lot more about me than you probably even wanted to." The comment came off flippantly, but he picked up on the serious undercurrent in her tone. He'd seen that dozens of times, too. A regular law-abiding citizen who suddenly finds themselves on the wrong side of crime. It was shocking and could completely throw them off balance. Totally understandable under the circumstances and another reason he liked making her laugh and breaking down some of the shock.

"What made you decide to adopt?" Not that he thought there was anything wrong with it. Taking a baby into her home was admirable. He found that he was curious about *her* decision in particular and wanted to know more about what made Renee tick.

"There were a lot of reasons. I guess in the end I realized I wanted to start my family and that no longer meant being traditional about it. Any time I brought up the subject of putting down roots and starting a family to my ex, he got squirrely about it. The crazy thing is that we'd just lived together so long marriage and family seemed like the next logical step. Being with him became a routine. Then, suddenly, I pulled into the parking lot of the place where we both worked in different departments. My life with him flashed before my eyes and I started crying. Like really crying and I am so not a crier. I didn't want to go inside the building. I didn't want to go home. It was crazy because I felt like we had already made this commitment to each other that we had to honor, and we weren't even married. We'd never even made our relationship official. When his lease was up five years ago after we'd been dating for two years, he asked what I thought about saving on rent and him moving in with me. I remember shrugging my shoulders and telling him that would be fine. There was nothing romantic or special about it. It felt like a business exchange. Isn't that weird?"

"So many people settle for less. It's easier to stay together than to break up after a certain point." He'd been in a similar relationship early on. "I dated someone once who, despite using serious precautions, told me she was pregnant with my child."

"What did you do?" Renee's hand came up to her mouth to cover her shock.

"Stuck around. There was no way I could walk away from my own child. There were rumors circulating that she'd been unfaithful on more than one occasion when I had cases that had me out of town for days on end. The relationship seemed to be winding down when she turned up pregnant, which left a few unanswered questions in my mind. I held off on the marriage until I was certain the child was mine. He wasn't." Those last two words had never made him feel so raw before. Damned if he hadn't stuffed those emotions down deep and tried his level best to forget. Talking about it now with Renee made him able to dredge up the past.

"I'm sorry." Her compassion shed a spark of light in the darkest places in his soul. It wasn't so much that he'd wanted to have a child with Stephanie as it was the loss of the kid he'd believed might be his.

"Thank you. It means more than you know to hear you say that." He meant those words. Cash tried to convince himself that he was sharing personal information with Renee to help her relax. It wasn't true. He liked talking to her and wanted to get to know her better. Part of that process was giving up a little about himself. But it was time to shift the conversation back to her. "What did you do while sitting in the car? Did you decide to go to work? Stay with him longer?"

"I knew in that moment the relationship was over for me. Does it sound crazy?"

"Not in the least. It's easy to stay with someone out of habit. It's easy to get comfortable." Cash could relate. He was pretty damn careful not to send mixed signals to the women he'd dated after Stephanie. He never would've moved in with someone he didn't have the intention to marry. Not because he was taking some moral high road, it just seemed like that meant he would already be committed. He'd seen a couple of his brothers go down that road only to have it bite them afterward. It was an easy mistake to make.

"Considering the fact that I was a leaky faucet, there was no way I could go to work. I texted my boss and said that I needed to take a sick day. Instead of going home, I went to this park near our apartment. I lost track of time sitting there in my car, watching kids play on the playground equipment. I was transfixed." She breathed out a heavy sigh. "I resolved to get my act together right then and there. Having a family was important to me. Having a husband was not. Eventually, I got the nerve to go home. But before I could end the relationship, Jamison got the call about his mother. Her doctor gave her six months to live. She survived for a year. I couldn't walk away under those circumstances with a clean conscience. Color me the fool."

"It's not foolish to be kind. Jamison sounds

like a selfish jerk who doesn't deserve someone like you." Cash couldn't help but come to her defense when he saw how much she was beating herself up over her decision to stay long after she stopped caring for her ex. "It shows incredible courage to stick around in a situation like that."

Renee took a minute to respond, like she wanted to really digest the words he'd just spoken. Her gaze lifted to his and there was something unexpected in her eyes, a spark that hadn't been there before. Frustration turned into vulnerability. Vulnerability quickly changed to something else altogether…desire?

In the space of a few seconds, the room heated and that spark in her eyes sent electricity shooting through him, seeking an outlet. A small explosion detonated in the center of his chest and Cash knew in that moment just how much trouble he was in when it came to the single mother.

Chapter Eight

Renee could get lost in Cash's steel eyes. She knew the instant her world had tilted on its axis and she'd stopped fighting the attraction she felt toward Cash—an attraction that had nearly bowled her over from the minute she'd opened the door to find him standing on her porch.

Having strong feelings for someone she barely knew should be odd, not comfortable, not like it was the most natural thing. Reminding herself they'd barely met did nothing to quell the squall gaining steam inside her. And yet, she'd known Jamison for almost a year before they'd started dating and look how that had turned out.

Looking back, it had been Jamison's persistence that had won her over. She'd listened to her head when it had said a man who kept after her for a date for a solid year would be there for her in the long run. It was almost comical when she looked back at their relationship.

A thought struck. Had she traded love for security? If she had, the joke was on her.

The sizzle of attraction and longing that she felt for Cash was foreign. But then, Renee never would've allowed herself to truly fall for anyone no matter how much she tried to convince herself that she liked them. Or was that just the lie she'd told herself to protect her own heart?

Being with Cash had her questioning all her beliefs about love. Because somewhere along the line, she'd convinced herself that true love was about sacrifice and digging her heels in to stay with someone because he needed her without regard for how little she got in return. Had she settled with Jamison?

The real answer was a slap of reality. In a word…yes. She'd settled for someone who needed her rather than hold out for the person who stirred feelings she wasn't certain how to handle. This out-of-control feeling she had in Cash's presence freaked her out more than she wanted to acknowledge.

Keeping a handle on her emotions was how she'd survived her childhood. As much as she wanted to lean into the feeling of being near Cash, it was too much, too fast.

The buzz of his cell phone broke into the moment happening between them. He checked the screen before glancing up. This time when they made eye contact, she could keep her emotions in check. Barely. Her cheeks flushed at how transparent she was being. The man had just shared something very personal with her and in the process made her feel special. How special was she to him?

Cash O'Connor worked in law enforcement. His job would make him good at getting people to trust him. Clearly, he was good at his job because she'd gone all in for a few minutes with him. She blinked and leaned back in her chair, trying to regain more of her composure—composure that was a slippery slope around this man.

"Colton has a couple of interviews lined up for early tomorrow morning, starting with the crew leader from your moving company." He glanced up at her after double-checking his screen.

Renee's heart jackhammered the inside of her rib cage, slamming out a staccato rhythm. She needed a break from the heat pinging between them and figured it would die down on its own as she spent more time with him. So far, it was a rising tide turning into one helluva wave ready to crash into shore. "We should get a few hours of sleep."

Cash responded to the text before catching her gaze. A warning shot straight to her heart with the look on his face. He put his hands up in the surrender position. "I think I already know the answer to this but I wanted you to think about leaving Abby at the ranch. It might be safer for her here with Stacy."

"She's safest with her mother." Those words rolled off her tongue so easily they gave a boost to her confidence as a new parent.

"I thought you might say that." He quirked a devastating grin and a look that seemed an awful lot like approval. "Let's grab a few hours of sleep and we'll head out at first light."

RENEE WAS SURPRISINGLY able to nod off for a few hours. Abby woke at first light, so Renee retraced her steps to the kitchen to make a bottle. Cash sat at the table, staring at the screen of his laptop.

"Did you sleep?" she asked.

"Enough." He immediately got up and helped make the formula. They worked as a team and when Abby had been tended to, Renee put her daughter on a blanket that was on the floor of the guest room long enough to freshen up.

She gathered baby supplies and then returned to the kitchen where Cash handed her a bagel.

"Shall we?" he asked after she polished it off.

She nodded before following him to his vehicle where he brought a to-go coffee for her. She couldn't think of a safer place than a sheriff's office, so she felt confident in her decision to bring Abby along. Besides, the little girl wasn't leaving Renee's sight. This child would know how much her mother loved her. Once this ordeal was behind the two of them, Renee planned to shower her daughter with what kids needed most—unconditional love and acceptance.

After securing Abby's seat in the back, Renee climbed into the passenger side and buckled in. Maybe it was the moment that had happened between them a few hours ago that seemed to linger, but she wanted to know more about Cash O'Connor. Since she had no idea where to start, she folded her hands in her lap and sat quietly.

Thankfully, he broke the silence. "Is your family originally from Dallas?"

"Yes. I grew up inside the Loop, which means Loop 12 if you're not familiar. My parents owned a resale shop south of the Trinity River. I worked there summers and after school, which taught me a lot about running a small family business. I also decided it wasn't for me so I now work for a global company."

"Really? What didn't you like about the small family business?" He started the engine and navigated onto the long driveway as the sun started to rise.

"I could tell you that a lot of it was because

of the long hours and no health insurance. You probably know best that family businesses basically means working all day and bringing work home. But, honestly, my parents fought all the time. When I think of owning a business, that's what comes to mind. Unhappiness. Arguments. Blaming. Screaming at each other. There was no way I was going to repeat their mistakes." She hadn't really thought about that until now. The realization hit home. It also struck her that she and Jamison rarely ever argued. In part because she had always been easygoing, but also because she let him have his way. What was there to fight about?

"It's important to be able to separate work from home." His comment made her thoughts shift to his situation. Now that his father was gone, would he be expected to step into the family business? It wasn't a question she felt she had the right to ask. But it must be on his mind. Then again, he'd thrown himself into her investigation. She got it. Work was a good distraction from grief and despair. Her work had been a saving grace getting her through that last year with Jamison. Despite Renee's challenging relationship with her parents, she'd loved them. Losing them both so suddenly had been the most difficult thing she'd ever had to deal with until recently.

"Your family seems to have their priorities in the right place. Not only do I admire them for it, I hope to emulate their example with my daughter." Jamison's mother had put her son before everything else. Renee wasn't bothered by the relationship at first. She had confused it with love back then. It wasn't until Jamison's mother had pulled Renee aside to say that her son had complained about Renee's almost constant nagging for him to pick up after himself around their apartment that she realized how unhealthy the relationship was. She'd been mortified. A quick decision was made right there and then. His mother didn't get to tell Renee what to do. And, besides, how awful was it that the person who should be her partner was doing nothing but complaining about her to his mother?

"Believe me when I say we know how fortunate we are. My parents married young and started a family soon after. I think they survived Caroline's kidnapping by making damn sure they always put us first. As strong as my mother is, I doubt she would've survived if she hadn't learned she was pregnant with me a few weeks after my sister was taken."

"I'm so sorry, Cash. I'd like to say that I can't imagine how that would feel and, truly, I count my blessings that Abby is in this back seat instead of..." She couldn't finish the sentence without getting so choked up she could barely breathe. What his mother, his family, went through was inconceivable. "After what we've been through in the past twenty-four hours, I can only imagine it's the tip of the iceberg compared to what your parents have endured. Bad things shouldn't happen to such good people."

"To be honest, I don't think my mother ever stopped looking for Caroline or hoping she'd show up one day out of the blue." The pain in his voice struck a chord. One event could change the course of someone's life so completely. The randomness of life hit home.

"Hope can be a beautiful and yet painful thing," she acknowledged.

"Truer words have never been spoken." He rocked his head and tightened his grip on the steering wheel. His voice softened when he said, "Thanks for listening to me talk about my family, by the way. You're the first person I've wanted to talk to about them."

"Thank you for trusting me, Cash." Hearing that he'd opened himself up to *her* and shared his pain with *her* sent another dangerous shot of warmth to her heart.

"I just thought you should know that you're special to me."

Renee's heart really beat double time hearing those words. She wanted to tell him that she felt the same more than anything. But the words died on her lips and all her defenses flared. What was wrong with her that she couldn't? How broken was she that she couldn't utter the words trying to form on her lips?

Instead of talking, which she'd never been all that good at anyway, she reached out and touched his arm.

One touch shouldn't bring so many parts of her to life—her body, her mind, her heart.

Saying that she was in trouble when it came to the devastating man sitting beside her would just be stating the obvious. Truly opening herself up would require more than desire, more than heat so intense it pinged between them even now. She *wanted* to be able to let her emotions take over and go with the feelings pulsing inside her. But she couldn't.

The tapes embedded so deep in the back of her mind played a different message. They sent a warning. They told her that every relationship would end up like her parents' toxic one. They said everyone would eventually let her down. They said that she couldn't really trust another soul.

Her situation with Jamison was sad. She felt a fool for staying longer than she should've. But a man like Cash could devastate her if she got into a relationship with him and it ended. And considering she was no good at relationships, it would end.

Renee withdrew her hand and apologized.

"Why are you sorry?" The hurt in his voice put another chink in her carefully constructed armor.

"I just am."

CASH COULD FEEL the temperature in the cab change the minute Renee pulled her hand back. Had he done something wrong?

The fact that he'd wanted to talk to her about his family and his past still shocked him. He tried to convince himself that he was putting his witness at ease by sharing a common bond. The voice inside his head—the one that didn't put up with any snow job he tried to sell—called him out.

He'd opened up to Renee because he felt a connection to her unlike anything he'd ever experienced with another person. Instead of acknowledging how special she was, he took another route. Cash decided that he was ready to deal with the events from the past. This case was good for him, he reasoned. It caused him to confront his demons so he could move on. Maybe he was ready to unpack the past and move on from it…trust again.

The situation with Pops had Cash twisted up

emotionally. There was no way he could deal with losing his father without first reconciling the loss of his sister, Caroline. And he'd searched cold case files for years…still did… with the hope that one day he'd be able to bring closure for his parents. Now that Pops was gone, the opportunity was lost with him.

It was like a bullet slammed into Cash at the thought. The man he'd put on a pedestal and respected his entire life was gone. A heavy blanket dropped on his shoulders.

Dammit. Dammit. Dammit.

Rather than wallow in the feeling, Cash put it into perspective. His mother needed him to be strong. His brothers needed someone to lead them. Well, that thought was almost comical. His brothers were grown men. Still, being the eldest, he sometimes saw his siblings as his responsibility. Either way, Cash's feelings came in a hard third. Stuffing his emotions into the box he was so good at finding, he tucked it away and refocused on the case in front of him.

After a long silence, he pulled into a parking spot at his brother's office. Caroline was on his mind. He didn't regret talking about his sister with Renee even though discussing her at all with someone outside the family wasn't done. "I told you about what happened to my sister because I wanted you to know that you're not alone. Caroline was taken from her crib in my parents' old house—"

"Hold on a second. Didn't you say she was the same age as Abby when it happened?" Renee asked.

"Yes. Before you get too riled up it has been more than three decades since Caroline went missing with no other similar crimes in or near Katy Gulch in between. There have been cases of parent abductions of babies around the same age, but none reported with a child being taken from his or her crib, and no cases of someone trying twice." He'd already thought about the other incidences because he knew this one would dredge up painful old memories for his mother. He'd read the cold case file on his sister. All living relatives had been interviewed, some several times. As an investigator, it made sense to him that the focus would be on next of kin. More than three quarters of abductions involved a parent. Stranger abductions accounted for less than one percent of cases. And those were some of the least recoverable.

"Part of me hoped no one close to me could be this cruel. I guess that might not be the case." Her chin jutted out with what seemed to be determination. "Guess I have to get used to the reality there are bad people in the world."

"The birth mother might have changed her

mind. You already heard that the attorney you used to adopt has been linked to a few questionable adoptions. We'll have a better idea of what's going on after hearing from suspects in the interviews."

Renee nodded before climbing out of the passenger seat and opening the back door to take Abby out of her car seat.

"Can I help with anything?" He wanted to lighten her load in any way he could.

"Would you mind taking the diaper bag?" she asked.

"Not a bit." He made a move to pick it up from the floorboard when he thought she was taking a step back. Signals crossed and she ended up leaning into the vehicle at the same time as him. Their shoulders bumped and more of that electricity shot through him. He suppressed a small smile. The electricity pinging between them was inconvenient. Although he told himself it was good on some level. It meant his heart was capable of taking the leap with someone, at least. Getting to know Renee did little to tamp down his attraction. If anything, her intelligence made her that much more physically appealing.

He backed up first. "Go ahead."

She smiled at him as she took a step back. "Sorry. I was trying to help you."

"Since your hands are full, how about I do the honors?"

"Deal." Seeing the way she beamed at the little girl in her arms made the image of a family come to mind. After his experience with Stephanie, he didn't consider himself the settling down type.

One of Cash's uncles had lived perfectly fine without a wedding band. Uncle Brady had made the choice never to wed and had lived his life on the ranch until sickness took him too young. At fifty, he'd dated the same woman for a decade and neither had felt the need to live under the same roof or go before the Justice of the Peace.

Cash could see himself in a similar arrangement. At least, he could until he'd met Renee and Abby. The two of them were carving out a special place in his heart. Again, he told himself being open to the possibility of one day meeting and falling in love with someone who made him want the whole package was a positive. Commitment had just seemed so permanent to him before. There'd never been a person he'd want to wake up to every day—day after day—without getting bored or needing a change. Also, he considered himself married to a job that would always come first. Most of his early relationships proved what his brother had learned the hard way. Law enforcement jobs and long-term personal relationships weren't always a good mix.

He'd dated a few women who'd convinced themselves they could go the distance if things got serious. The attitude lasted, on average, three months. The first time he'd miss an event special to his girlfriend, an attitude shift occurred by the next date. He'd learned the hard way the countdown to the end of the relationship began at that point. His relationships were predictable. He had it down to a science.

Abby cooed, blew spit bubbles and gave Cash the biggest smile he'd ever seen. The kid was all big eyes and cuteness. "You have quite the charmer there."

Renee's cheeks warmed as she looked at Abby. "I'm going to have to keep an eye on this one when she turns fifteen."

"I'll help you find a stick to beat the boys away." His joke was met with a genuine laugh and he realized what it could imply—that he would be there when Abby turned fifteen. Instead of thinking too deeply about that, he put his hand on the small of Renee's back as the two walked into his brother's office building.

Chapter Nine

The minute they stepped inside the lobby, Gert Francis rounded her desk to greet them. His brother's secretary was in her late sixties and could be best described as lively. She had a twinkle to her brown eyes and a grandmotherly smile that was disarming. Folks had nicknamed her Oprah for her ability to get people to open up like the popular TV host, Oprah Winfrey.

Gert threw her arms around Cash first and brought him into a sincere hug. "Stacy called the minute she could. I'm so sorry to hear about your daddy."

"Thank you, Gert." He was still trying to process the fact Pops was gone. "Your sympathy means a lot."

When she looked up at him, tears streaked her cheeks. She pulled back and squeezed his forearm. "I've already said this to Colton, but I want you to hear it, too. You let me know if your family needs anything and I mean *anything*. You hear?"

"Yes, ma'am." Her kindness was greatly appreciated. She'd worked for the last sheriff before he'd retired and Colton had been elected. She'd been a valuable team member, helping Colton get up to speed on his job. They'd known her for years but she'd become like family since he'd taken over as sheriff.

"I already told Stacy that I'm making a casserole to drop off at the ranch after work," Gert said matter-of-factly. She was the roll-up-her-sleeves type. Her husband had passed away five years ago. Since she'd suffered the same loss as his mother, she would be a good person to lean on for advice on how to get through the coming days.

"Mother will appreciate your good cooking and your company." Talking to Gert was making his father's death more real. Cash had been able to put his emotions on hold, allowing himself to get wrapped up in Renee's case. He didn't dare open the floodgates now. "You know how special you are to our family."

Warmth radiated from her when she looked up at him and then to Renee.

"You must be Renee. I'm Gert." She was devoted to Colton and to the county. When she wasn't at work, she watched a constant stream of popular police and detective shows. Her quick wit proved helpful in many cases—cases that she liked to try to solve before Colton. Being sheriff in a ranching community meant crime that mostly involved missing pets, bicycles and rowdy teenagers who were blowing off steam in cow pastures. Hard crime was rare in Katy Gulch and the surrounding community. Although, it did happen. Case in point, his sister's kidnapping. Although, that was more than thirty years ago. Still, he feared this was the tip of the iceberg. His fear came from instinct honed by years of training and experience.

"Very nice to meet you, Gert," Renee said, her fingers tight around the carrier holding Abby.

Cash had never seen Gert pass up an opportunity to ask to hold a baby. She seemed to realize that Renee wouldn't let go of her child after what had happened.

"I'm real sorry about what you and your sweet angel are going through. We have some of the best lawmen in the state working on your case. Katy Gulch is a better community than this, a safe community." Gert prided herself on living in a place where people helped each other. The sentiment had been built into ranchers and farmers since long before Cash was born and it was part of the reason he would never leave his hometown. Cash O'Connor was right where he belonged.

"Thank you." Renee said the words on a small sigh. She smiled and he could've sworn those words put her more at ease than he'd seen her so far.

"I don't want to keep you. Colton said to bring you straight to the interview room and then let him know when you're there. Follow me," Gert said.

The lobby had Gert's desk on the left and a long counter on the right. There were glass doors that required a special ID badge directly in front of them. Once behind those doors, the building was shaped like a U. Colton's office was to the right and down the hall. The route to the interview room was behind another locked door to their left.

Cash brought up the rear as Gert led Renee through the locked doors and down the hallway to the witness room, which was roughly the size of a walk-in closet.

Abby was busy blowing raspberries on her fist. The minute Renee stepped inside the room, she froze. In barely a whisper, she asked, "Can he hear us?"

"No." Cash kept his voice low.

The lights were dim and there was a small speaker with a box and a button. The button was used to communicate orders to the people inside the interview room, which was on the other side of the two-way mirror.

Gert turned tail. Before she disappeared, she said, "I'll let your brother know that you're in here and you're good to go."

"Thank you," Cash said.

Studying the man sitting down at a metal table, she confirmed the identity of her moving crew's chief. "That's the guy who introduced himself as Paul."

A few minutes later, Colton joined them. "I wanted to stop in here before the interview to see if you recognize this man."

"Yes, that's Paul."

"Paul Miser," Colton confirmed. "According to Gert, he has a clean record with no known priors. He's not a college student." No one seemed surprised about that despite the moving company's name, College Boy Movers. "But he has been working for the company five years. Got moved up to crew chief two years ago. He supports his mother, who is on disability."

Cash wasn't surprised Gert was able to dig all that up in a matter of hours. The woman worked magic.

"His girlfriend is six months pregnant," Colton continued. That pretty much ruled Paul out for personal reasons in Cash's book but he still wanted to hear what the suspect had to say. There was still a possibility that a person with a kid on the way might be desperate for cash. A deep dive into the guy's financials could clear up whether he needed money or not. Of course, Colton couldn't just dig into someone's bank account without a warrant but that didn't mean he couldn't ask permission. Innocent people usually volunteered information to help a case and a guy with a kid on the way might be more cooperative in an attempted kidnapping investigation.

"Your job was the only one he and his crew had. He says he arrived home afterward and took a nap on the couch. His mother woke him in time for dinner and he was home after that. His mother corroborated the story that he was alone in his room. She doesn't work, so he lives there to help her with her bills. His girlfriend's job is too far away so she lives with her family through the week. However, the mother went to bed at eight thirty and didn't see him again until nine o'clock the next morning."

"Not exactly an ironclad alibi," Cash observed.

"No, it isn't."

"Let's see what Mr. Miser has to say." Colton excused himself and closed the door behind him. He strode into the interview room with an entirely different demeanor. Shoulders stiff, he introduced himself to Paul Miser. Paul was solidly built. Most would describe him as stocky. He had on a short-sleeved company T-shirt with dark denim jeans and tennis shoes. His brown hair was almost military short, his eyes were serious and his forehead had deep worry lines for a young man. He carried himself with dignity. Cash's training and experience made him good at reading people. Granted, there were times when he was wrong but those were rare.

The minute Colton had entered the room, Paul stood and readied himself for a handshake. On first appraisal, Paul Miser didn't seem to be the jerk they were looking for.

After introductions were made, Colton got right to the point.

"Where were you this morning, Mr. Miser?" Colton asked, motioning toward the chairs.

"Home." Paul took a seat across the table from Colton, then leaned forward and rested his elbows on the table with his hands clasped. His body language signified that he was nervous and ready to cooperate. "My mother's house, that is."

"Can you confirm her home is located in Big Rock, Texas?" Colton asked.

"Yes, sir." The location in Big Rock would

make it impossible for him to be in Katy Gulch during the second kidnapping attempt.

Even though Paul was looking less and less like a suspect, he might be able to provide valuable information about his crew and especially the mystery mover.

"Can anyone verify your whereabouts this morning?" Colton asked the missing piece, which was for someone besides his mother to corroborate his whereabouts.

"My mother was home," Paul stated.

"Is she the only person you saw?" Colton asked.

Paul shook his head. "No, sir. My fiancée stopped by before her shift."

"What time was that?" Colton leaned back in his chair, a sure sign Paul had moved from suspect to witness in his eyes.

"Around seven o'clock." All Colton needed to do to clear Paul was verify the information.

Using two fingers, Colton pushed a pad of paper and a pen over to where Paul could easily use them. "Can you write down her name and contact information for me, sir?"

Paul obliged.

"Thank you." Colton took the offering and motioned for a deputy to come inside. Deputy Sal Frank entered the room as Colton ripped off the top sheet. He held out the piece of paper.

"Can you give this to Gert and ask her to call the number and verify that Mr. Miser was home this morning?"

"Yes, sir," Sal said before taking the name and leaving the room. The door closed behind him with a soft clink. He'd been a deputy for ten years when Colton took the job as sheriff. Sal was a respected and trusted colleague.

"It says on your company's website that all employees are bonded and insured." He turned his attention back to Paul.

"We are." His right heel tapped against the concrete flooring.

"Does your company bond and insure its employees?" Colton asked.

"Yes, sir. It does. I sometimes send people in to HR to interview. Some of them get the green light. Others don't make the cut. I don't have anything to do with that part of the process."

Colton nodded. His relaxed body posture seemed to be putting Paul more at ease. "Do you always work with the same crew?"

"Yes, sir. Most of the time. Occasionally we'll get a last-minute sub like on the other morning's job. One of my regulars came down with the flu. So, I got a sub. He's the younger cousin of one of the owners."

"You have a name for this guy?" Colton again moved the pen and paper to Paul.

"All I know is his first name, Jo-Jo."

"Do you know if Jo-Jo is a smoker?"

Paul cocked his head to the side. "No, sir. I didn't see him light anything up and I don't know much about him personally."

"So you didn't see him with a lighter at any point?"

"Not him. But I lost my Zippo. Did someone find it?" He looked Colton in the eyes and then glanced away. Making eye contact with the investigator gave Paul a little more credibility in Cash's book.

"The lighter belongs to you?" Colton maintained his relaxed composure and Cash realized it was taking some effort. He knew his brother well. The connection to the Zippo was important. Or so they'd thought. If Paul's alibi checked out—and he fully believed that it would—that piece of evidence was no good.

"Yes, sir. I quit smoking a long time ago. The Zippo belonged to my father, who passed away ten years ago. He'd had it made special with a dragon on it. He loved dragons and had one just like it on his motorcycle jacket. He wasn't a bad guy. He never got into any gangs. He liked to ride his Harley on Sundays." The Zippo's importance in the investigation just dropped down a few notches. As long as Paul's whereabouts could be confirmed, he was in the clear, anyway. Besides, it had been a little too much to hope that the lighter they'd found on the site would be able to clear up the case. It happened. This just didn't seem to be one of those cases based on Paul's statement.

It was probably safe to cross Paul off the suspect list. The sub on his moving crew, Jo-Jo, might be another story. Considering he was related to the owners of the company, he shouldn't be too difficult to track down.

Renee moved closer to Cash without taking her eyes off Paul. "Do you think he's telling the truth?"

"I do. And his story will be easy enough to verify," Cash supplied. "I had hoped the lighter might lead us to the perp. Doesn't look like that's the case here. It must've slipped out of Paul's pocket during the move, which would explain why we found it near the ladder next to the side of the house."

"Sounds like an important family heirloom. I'm sure he would've backtracked and contacted me sooner or later to see if I'd found it." Her observation skills were dead on.

"What do you think about Jo-Jo?" Her voice was practically a whisper.

"If the story of him being a relative turns out to be true, I have my doubts that he'd be stupid enough to commit a crime on a job he can be linked to. Don't get me wrong, I've seen worse, but it's unlikely. We'll follow the trail anyway and see where it leads." Cash felt like he'd seen or heard it all when it came to crime and criminals, but he'd probably only scratched the surface in his decade-long career in law enforcement.

In the interview room, Colton thanked Paul before instructing Sal to escort the witness out of the building.

When it was clear, Colton opened the door and came into the room with Renee and Cash.

"I'd like to hear your assessment," Colton said to Cash. The two ran scenarios by each other from time to time when a fresh set of eyes was needed on a case. In his view, that might be overkill with this witness, but Colton was obviously dotting every i and crossing every t. Cash relayed the same thing he'd told Renee. Colton rocked his head the entire time, indicating his agreement.

"What's your take on Jo-Jo?" Colton asked when Cash was finished.

"Probably the same as yours," Cash said. "He'd be too stupid to commit the crime on his cousin's dime."

"Agreed." Before Colton could continue, Gert appeared in the doorway.

"Okay if I interrupt, sir?" she asked Colton.

He waved her in.

"Mr. Miser's story checks out with his fiancée. She confirmed that he was home on the morning in question at seven a.m. when she stopped by to see him before her shift. She said his bedroom is in the front of the house and his mother's is in the back, so his mother wouldn't know one way or the other if he had visitors. She offered her employer's name and number to verify that she had to be at work at seven thirty, which I called and verified that she had been."

"Looks like his story checks out. Great work, Gert. Thank you." Colton's compliment elicited a satisfied smile from Gert. She took great pride in her investigative work and it showed. She was thorough, and Cash would have her on his team any day.

"Let me know if you need anything else," she said with a wink. She also had the ability to brighten any room with her spunky personality.

Colton handed her the notepad with Jo-Jo's name along with the name of the moving company on it. "Mind finding out who this guy is? His cousin is one of the owners. We need to track down his whereabouts from this morning."

"On it, sir." Her eyes sparked at the new assignment. "I just got a call from Deputy Mark Ernest and there's something you should know." Her excitement was replaced by concern. "Would you mind stepping into the hallway and closing the door?"

Cash's interest peaked.

"Certainly." Colton glanced at Renee before shooting an apologetic look to his brother. "I'll be back as soon as I know what this is about."

What was so important it needed to be discussed out of earshot and in the middle of an investigation? Cash would dismiss it as having nothing to do with Abby's attempted abduction except the look on Gert's face threw him for a loop.

"Everything okay?" Renee seemed to pick up on the distress in Gert's voice.

"I guess we'll both know in a few minutes."

Chapter Ten

Renee gently bounced Abby. There was no way she was handing her daughter over to anyone else even though the child was as heavy as a bowling ball at this point and she could use a break.

Colton knocked on the door before opening it. His facial muscles were tense and the worry lines on his forehead seemed deeper. He and his brother exchanged a worried look and the knot that had formed in Renee's chest tightened.

Abby started working up to fuss, interrupting the moment. "Maybe she's bored."

In the short time Abby had been her daughter, Renee was starting to get a feel for her daughter's needs. Granted, she had a long way to go before she would feel confident, but this was progress and she'd take any she could get when it came to motherhood.

"Might want to take a walk. We'll be more comfortable in my office where we can close the door and talk." Colton's tone of voice tightened the knot even more.

She followed Colton, who took the lead.

"Do you want to wait in my brother's office while I grab a cup of coffee?" Cash asked in the hallway in front of his brother's office.

Renee didn't want to be rude, but she'd rather stick with Cash. Being near him had a calming effect on her and she could use all the good vibes she could get. "Mind if I come with you?"

"I have a phone call to make anyway." Colton gave her an out and she'd take it.

Cash nodded before continuing down the hall. He stepped into a small break room that had a kitchenette with dual coffeepots like the kind in a restaurant. They reminded her of the years she'd waited tables in college. Other than those, there were two high-top tables with three chairs tucked underneath each.

He went to work grabbing a clean cup and filling it with fresh coffee. She watched as the cotton of his light blue button-down shirt stretched over his muscles with his every move. The guy was muscles and strength, and…sex appeal. Yeah. There it was. He was gorgeous and she knew this was the worst possible time to notice or care. But unfamiliar feelings were building inside her—feelings that should scare the hell out of her.

Except that everything about Cash O'Connor was different. She was curious to see what that meant. With a new baby, new house and new town, she wasn't looking to add any complications to her life. She almost laughed out loud. Life seemed to be doing just fine throwing complications at her without extra help.

And, of course, she'd meet an honest, caring and intelligent man at this point. Because it made no sense in her life.

Renee sighed sharply as Abby made her hunger known, now having worked up to a real cry. The baby tried stuffing her fist in her mouth and missed more than anything. She also started rooting. Her daughter's tears were just about the most heartbreaking things Renee had ever seen.

Cash asked a colleague to grab one of Abby's formula bottles from his vehicle before he moved to the table and offered Renee a fresh cup of coffee.

"Thank you. You've been really great with Abby and me." Renee managed a genuine smile.

"I already told you about Colton's twins. To be honest, it's been a minute since I fed either one of them, though." He wiped a hand over his face and muttered a curse. "I gotta be a better uncle than that."

"They're lucky to have you. It's sad to say that I almost forgot about them considering evcrything that's been going on." She blew out a breath and figured she looked about as rough as she felt. A renegade strand of hair managed to get caught in her right eyelash. She blew at it to no avail. With both hands on Abby, she couldn't manage to get the hair off her eyelash and it was bugging the heck out of her.

"May I?" Cash locked gazes with her and her heart fluttered in her chest like a teenager on her first crush.

"Please."

He tucked the loose tendril behind her ear. His hand lingered there just long enough for more of that warmth she felt whenever he was near to circulate through her.

"Better?" he asked.

"Much." She heard the huskiness in her own voice. Staring into his steel eyes, she saw something that stirred a place deep inside her, a place that had been long neglected. Forgotten? There was a primal need in his gaze that brought out the same in her. Again, she cursed the timing of meeting him. Life could be so frustrating.

Yeah, her attraction to Cash was inconvenient. It was also a force unto itself that seemed impossible to set aside. There was also something hugely right about being this close to him, so close she could breathe in his masculine and spicy scent.

A noise in the hallway broke into the moment. One corner of his mouth upturned in a small smile before he took a step back and crossed muscled arms over a broad chest. The cotton of his shirt did that stretchy thing again. She forced herself to look away.

Renee expected someone to walk into the room but the person must've changed course or gone into one of the offices or small conference rooms. Renee reluctantly stood up. She wobbled and Cash's strong hand held her steady.

The deputy Cash had sent for the bottle returned. Renee prepared it then fed and changed her daughter, grateful for Cash's spontaneous help. The man could tape a diaper. The three of them returned to Colton's office. He'd been studying his computer screen until Cash interrupted him by knocking on his doorjamb.

Colton glanced over at them before waving them in. The fact that he didn't answer sent her pulse racing.

He stood up and motioned toward the leather couch and chairs on the other side of his expansive and neatly ordered office. She also noticed that he closed the door before joining them.

When he sat down after she and Cash took seats on the sofa and chair respectively, he leaned forward and rested his elbows on his knees. He clasped his hands together, and then he stared at the carpet for a long moment like he was searching for the right words.

Renee's heart was in her throat by the time he looked up again. Instead of focusing on her, his gaze was fixed on his brother.

"Ruth Hubert was found murdered in her garden." Colton's voice was low as his gaze dipped to Abby and back.

Cash stood up and started pacing. "She moved to the outskirts of town a few months before our sister was kidnapped. Years later, we reviewed the case files and found out that she'd been interviewed multiple times. The sheriff at the time seemed to believe she'd brought bad blood to town. It was also believed for a time that she was using her remote location to traffic people through the area." Cash stopped long enough to rake his fingers through his hair and then rub the day-old stubble on his chin. He shifted his attention to his brother. "What happened?"

"GSW to the back of the head."

Even she realized *GSW* meant *gunshot wound*, although she figured he was using the acronym to soften the news in front of her.

Cash's hands fisted at his sides. "Did I hear that right?"

His brother nodded.

"So, you're telling me that she was killed

execution-style in her garden?" Cash held his brother's gaze, waiting for confirmation. She understood the need for repetition. Hearing the news made her sick to her stomach.

"Afraid so." Colton blew out a sharp breath. "Sal is the one who saw her on his nightly rounds. He always checks on the houses of Katy Gulch's most remote residents. Even though Ms. Hubert lives on the outskirts of town, he makes a point to drive by her property at least once a week. She's not the friendly type so he just makes sure different lights are on if he's there in the evenings."

"Any relation to Renee's case?" Those words were daggers to the heart and Renee realized she'd been holding her breath, waiting for the answer.

Colton didn't immediately speak. Then came, "Sal checked her phone, which had been kicked off the porch, to see if there was an ICE." Renee knew that meant an *in case of emergency* contact. Colton delivered a bomb next. "Most of her contacts had no names. They were just phone numbers."

"Did he recognize any?" Cash made another lap around the room.

"Yes, he did." Colton shot an apologetic look toward Renee. "There was one. Kipp McGee."

Renee gasped. Hearing her lawyer's name in

the context of this conversation sent a mix of fear and anger swirling through her. Questions assaulted her. What if her lawyer was responsible for murder? What if her lawyer was the one who'd sent someone to snatch Abby back after the adoption? And then the question that nearly gutted her came... What if Abby's adoption was illegal and she was taken away for good?

Renee couldn't possibly lose the little girl who'd been born in her heart so many years ago and was now very much alive in her arms. It didn't matter that Abby had come into Renee's life only recently because the moment she'd held that little girl in her arms, she'd given her heart away forever.

"HIS NAME SEEMS to be coming up a lot lately." Cash moved next to Renee as she cradled her little girl. Based on her reaction and the look on her face that dared anyone to try to take her daughter away, he figured she was afraid she could lose Abby. Cash had four words for that scenario: *over his dead body.*

"It sure does," Colton agreed with a weary look.

Cash would do anything and everything in his power to ensure Abby stayed with Renee where she belonged. A few *what ifs* haunted him. What if the baby had been stolen from the birth mother? What if the birth mother gave consent for the adoption and then changed her mind? The other *what ifs* were more cut-and-dried. What if the birth mother wanted nothing to do with her child and handed her over for an illegal adoption? What if a higher bidder came along? What if McGee got Renee involved in a sketchy adoption that could result in her losing Abby? One look at the mother-daughter duo said Renee had gone all in with the child.

He hoped it wouldn't come down to a situation where Abby could legally be removed from Renee's home. He'd heard of a similar scenario happening and it was not only horrific but unfair to the adoptive parents.

The coroner would have to determine Ms. Hubert's time of death and they could start unpacking what the hell had happened. Colton buzzed Gert. "Can you get Kipp McGee here as soon as possible?"

"Yes, sir."

Gert buzzed back a few minutes later. "He's on his way."

"Really?" Colton sounded shocked. "So fast?"

"Let's just say that I convinced him it would be in his best interest to talk to you of his own accord. I sided with him and told him that he just needed to have a quick conversation to help clear up a misunderstanding."

"Remind me how good you are at your job before your next performance appraisal," Colton said. The joke lightened some of the heavy tension.

"Oh, I plan to," she quipped. "We might as well order lunch because it's a couple hours' drive for him."

CASH HAD TAKEN a turn holding Abby so that Renee could get a break. He'd even convinced her to take another nap on the sofa in Colton's office.

Gert knocked on the door, waking her.

"Kipp McGee is waiting to enter the interview room," she said. "There's a shortcut from my office across the courtyard. It'll be faster than circling around and we can get you in place before McGee is walked back." Colton was already at the door by the time Renee pushed up with her free arm.

She reached for her daughter and Cash brought her over immediately. Cash remembered when his nephews were around that age. They didn't seem heavy until he'd been carrying them for an hour. Then they became like lead weights in his arms. He'd offer to continue to carry Abby if it wasn't for the fierce look of determination on Renee's face. He understood her need to keep her daughter close. Hell, he didn't blame her one bit. The thought of having her little girl ripped out of her arms after she'd bonded with her was unimaginable.

Cash was familiar with the shorter path his brother took them on.

"I'll close the door," Colton said after stopping in the hallway to let them pass by to take position.

After thanking his brother, Cash leaned against the wall. He studied Renee, who looked exhausted. "Can I get you a chair?"

"That would be so nice." Her demeanor had changed and he noticed her shoulders were starting to sag. There were also dark circles under her eyes and she bit back a yawn. They could get through this one interview and then he'd offer to take her back to the ranch to get a break from his brother's office. Cash wanted to chew on the details of what they knew. Taking the rest of the night off would give Colton and his deputies a chance to dig deeper into the case.

Investigations took time. He had no idea if the Hubert case was connected to Renee's. Answers weren't likely tonight and especially now that resources would have to be reallocated to Ms. Hubert's place. And then there was all that was happening at home. Cash wanted to check on his mother and see how she was holding up.

A quick run next door and he netted one of the chairs from a conference room. He placed it directly in front of the two-way mirror a few seconds before he heard noise coming from down the hallway. He made a quick move to close the door, guarding their identities from her lawyer.

It was probably for the best that McGee didn't know his former client would be watching. Although, he might suspect someone was. This wasn't his first time in an interview room from the news Cash had read over the years. He'd heard the man's name mentioned repeatedly, but the two had yet to meet and a charge had yet to stick.

Kipp McGee wasn't the crisp-suit type that Cash had expected to see. The lawyer looked to be in his early forties and would be considered tall by average standards, maybe five feet, eleven inches. He had on a suit, dull gray in color, and his appearance could best be described as sloppy. One side of his white button-down shirt was untucked. He didn't wear a tie and the top couple of buttons were undone. He looked to be average weight except for his gut, which seemed a little overstuffed. His ruddy complexion gave him an aging amateur golfer or tennis player look, and his hair looked like it had been finger combed rather than brushed.

"Do you mind standing right here, Mr. McGee?" Colton pointed to a spot not five feet in across the mirror and directly in front of Renee. She flinched and leaned back in her chair as McGee moved into position.

Cash placed a hand on her shoulder to offer some measure of reassurance as he leaned toward the mirror and studied the lawyer. Much about his demeanor was disarming, except the slight twitch under his left eye.

"Right here?" McGee asked. On the surface, he looked eager to cooperate.

"Yes, sir." Colton always watched his p's and q's with a suspect and that wouldn't stop now. It was also one of the many things that had earned him a reputation as a one of the best in the state while still young in his career. He had a knack for reading people, knowing when to push and when to take a step back. As a fellow law enforcement officer and his brother, Cash couldn't be prouder.

"That's all. Thank you for your cooperation." Colton moved toward the table and chairs in the middle of the room.

McGee stared at the mirror a second longer than seemed appropriate, which was an odd thing for him to do. He had to realize he wouldn't be able to see who was standing on the other side.

Was the move meant to intimidate a victim or witness? Cash made note of the behavior and moved on. Granted, his opinion was tainted by the man's reputation—a reputation that, based on appearances, seemed to have been earned.

"How can I help you today, Sheriff?" McGee took the seat across the table from Colton. He took off his jacket and draped it over the back of his chair. Cash noticed sweat stains. If it hadn't been for the eye twitch and the fact the man had tried to stare into the mirror, Cash might have written the man off as harmless.

Paul Miser had claimed the dragon lighter. That piece of evidence no longer seemed to come into play, which was unfortunate. Forensics might have gotten lucky with prints. It had been less than twenty-four hours and that would increase their chances.

"I appreciate your willingness to cooperate," Colton began.

McGee's arms came up and he waved his hands in the air. His wide smile belied narrowed eyes. "Happy to oblige, sir."

Bet you are. McGee didn't come accompanied by another lawyer, which was strange but also seemed like a ploy to make him appear innocent.

"He seems different to me." Renee finally spoke up, her gaze still locked on to her lawyer. "It's like he's putting on a show to hide the fact that he's nervous."

"I agree."

Renee had keen observation skills.

"And he's working too hard. You know?" Her elbow accidentally touched his, sending more heat swirling from contact.

"It crossed my mind," Cash said.

She blew out a sharp breath. "Tell it to me straight. You're an officer of the law and I imagine you've seen or heard just about all there is to. What are my chances that I could lose Abby?"

"I'd like more than anything to say none, but I can't tell you that in good conscience."

There was no response, just a palpable sadness. When she turned to face him, her chin jutted out and her expression tensed. There was a whole helluva lot of determination there, too.

"I'll do right by Abby. Even if that means I have to give her up if it's best for her in the long run," she stated.

"We don't know if the adoption was illegal yet." It was important to follow evidence all the way through. Worrying beforehand—although he completely understood—wouldn't do anyone any good.

"True," she said on a sigh. "I'm just preparing myself for the worst. Don't get me wrong, I'll fight tooth and nail for this angel. But a few scenarios come to my mind that mean it wouldn't be right to keep her no matter how much she feels like my daughter already."

"You're an amazing mother—"

"How can you tell?" She blinked clear blue eyes at him.

"You're ready to put her above everything and everyone else, including yourself. She's barely been in your life and yet it's easy to see that you'd walk through fire for her." The fact that she smiled despite going through what must be one of the worst days of her life caused a thunderbolt to strike him in the center of the chest.

With those big beautiful eyes wide open, she thanked him.

Yeah, he was in trouble.

Chapter Eleven

"Can you account for your whereabouts for the past forty-eight hours?" Colton pushed the same notepad she'd recognized from earlier across the table. A pen rested on top.

Renee waited on the edge of her seat for the answer to that question.

Kipp made a show of being caught off guard by the question. His actions up to this point seemed very off to her compared to the confident lawyer she'd dealt with.

"Do I need to?" Kipp's expression morphed into shocked indignation.

"Yes, sir." Colton quickly added, "Purely in the spirit of cooperation."

"Okaaay." Kipp drew out the word. "I'm usually on phone calls throughout the day. I met with a client at lunch yesterday."

"What time exactly was that?" Colton leaned forward like he was hanging on the lawyer's every word.

"It was late. Around two o'clock." Kipp checked his wristwatch.

"Seems like an unusual time to eat lunch," Colton said.

"I go where my clients need me to. There are days when I work through lunch." Kipp's eyebrow shot up. "I'm sure you understand that."

"Yes, sir. I'm a little too familiar." Colton seemed to be trying to ease the tension. Even Renee could see that a wall had just come up.

Kipp leaned back in his chair and steepled his fingers.

"How did you qualify your lawyer?" Cash asked.

"I didn't. I took him at face value." She should've done more digging around, checked into his background a little more. It had never occurred to her that the adoption wasn't anything but aboveboard or that she could give her heart to a child only to have her ripped out of Renee's arms. It wasn't like she'd acted on impulse, either. She had been carefully considering having a family for years. Of course, she'd believed that she and Jamison would've been married first. A cold chill ran down her back at the thought of being trapped in a marriage with a partner like him.

Looking back, she had no regrets. If she'd walked away from Jamison while his mother was dying, Renee would have felt like an awful person. By the time his mother had passed away, Jamison's affair was out in the open.

There was no denying the fact that Renee had made a snap judgment on hiring her attorney, but she'd carefully thought out becoming a mother. It was something she'd wanted to do for years and maybe for her entire life.

Looking back on what had led up to the adoption wouldn't do any good. Renee refocused on the here and now. If there was an unwitting birth mother out there somewhere who'd had her child taken from her by anything other than her own free will, Renee would do the right thing by Abby and ensure the two were reconnected. After having her child nearly abducted in her own bedroom, Renee could imagine the horror a birth mother would go through to find her child missing.

"I'm sure you'll understand my need to respect the privacy of my clients," Kipp's voice cut through her heavy thoughts. Her mind was starting to spin out. She had always been an overthinker and this was a lot to chew on.

"Does that mean you won't provide the names of anyone who can verify where you've been in the past forty-eight hours, Mr. McGee?" Colton's voice caused the hair on the back of her neck to prick.

"No, sir. I will not." Kipp stood up and wrangled his arms into his suit jacket. His actions so far weren't flattering or instilling any confidence.

"Sir, if you don't mind, I'd like to ask one more question before you walk out of this interview." Colton didn't stand up but he nailed Kipp with his glare. His tone had switched to all business. Kipp straightened his back like he was preparing for a fight.

"Go right ahead. I don't have anything to hide." Renee wished with all her heart that was true. As much as she didn't want someone she knew to be responsible for terrorizing her and Abby, if her lawyer had done something illegal to push the boundaries then her life could drastically change. If Jamison or the creepy guy from the office was responsible, an arrest would solve the problem. The jerk would end up locked behind bars and Renee would be able to resume her new normal life with her daughter. But the lawyer on her adoption case...

She couldn't go there again because disaster was written all over the scenario involving McGee.

"What is your relationship with Ruth Hubert?" Colton asked. Renee picked up on the fact he hadn't used past tense even though the woman had been murdered in her garden.

Kipp glanced from the door to the mirror and then back to Colton. He rubbed a hand over his chin. "I don't have one." Kipp couldn't walk toward the exit any faster. He paused at the door but didn't turn around. "Now, if you'll excuse me. I'm late for a meeting in Houston."

"Do you travel around the state frequently for business?" Colton's eyebrow shot up.

"I go where work requires." McGee focused on the closed door.

"You're free to go. A deputy is waiting in the hallway to see you out." Colton rose to standing. "Mr. McGee."

Kipp stopped just outside the door. "Yes."

"Are you planning to travel outside of the state anytime in the near future?" Colton's question caused Kipp to bristle.

"No, sir." There was more than a hint of worry in his voice now.

"Good. Please let my office know if that changes." Colton's tone didn't waver.

"Yes, sir." Kipp couldn't get out of there fast enough.

"That's so not good," Renee said quietly.

Cash was by her side in the next beat, his reassuring hand on the small of her back.

"No, it wasn't." His steel voice was low. "You want to get out of here and head back to the ranch?"

"Yes, I do," Renee answered quickly. In fact, there was little else she wanted at the moment besides a safe place to unwind. She needed to get a permanent fix for Abby's window and hadn't done that yet. Lack of solid sleep was catching up to her and she was getting so tired her bones ached.

The door opened and Colton filled the frame. "The lawyer is gone. It's safe to come out now."

"It's been a long day. Renee agreed to take off with me so she can settle her daughter in and get some rest." The fact Cash so easily spoke of Abby as Renee's daughter brought more warmth to her heart. In a world that could be twisted and crazy and unexpected, that those words felt so right confirmed everything Renee had fought for in order to become a mother.

"I was just about to suggest the same. We're still trying to track down Mr. King and Ms. Tran." Colton rubbed the back of his hand over red-rimmed eyes. With one-year-old twins at home and a more-than-full-time job as sheriff, Renee could hardly imagine.

Cash embraced his brother in a hug and more of Renee's heart melted. She could learn a lot from these brothers about family, and part of her wished she would have the opportunity once this case was behind them. "Will you call if there's any change or news?"

"You know I will." Colton turned to Renee. "We'll do everything in our power to find the person responsible for both attempts." He didn't say kidnapping and she was grateful. Hearing the word spoken out loud brought back all those helpless feelings when she was caught off guard at home. The second time had been scary but she'd been more prepared. And determined.

Plus, there was something different about the second attempt. Granted, there were more people and the location was public. Was that why, looking back, she felt safer now? She had people around? People who cared about her and had her back?

"Thank you for everything you're doing," she said to Colton before kissing the top of Abby's head. "Becoming a mother is the greatest thing that's ever happened to me. I have every intention of doing whatever's necessary to keep her safe."

Colton nodded. "We promise to do the same. My office will be in touch."

"I'm taking them to the main house at the ranch," Cash informed his brother. Colton's eyebrow shot up but he didn't speak. "I'd like her to be around people and the ranch is the safest place I can think of until she gets her bedroom window fixed and a security system installed. I'm getting Russell on the job. He's the best, but he's also booked solid. He said he'd fit her in soon, but he might be calling last minute."

"Sounds like a good plan," Colton agreed.

Cash held his hand out toward the door and locked eyes with Renee. "Shall we?"

She retraced their earlier steps to his brother's office with Cash right behind her. Colton's secretary was on a call. She put her hand over the phone. "Nice meeting you."

She smiled and waved as they moved through the lobby. After securing Abby's car seat, Renee shook her arms to get some feeling back in them. Both had gone numb more than an hour ago. She climbed into the passenger seat and buckled in.

"Are you okay with going back to my family's ranch?" he asked. "I'd offer to stay at your place but with everything going on with my family I'd like to check in at home. We can stay at the main house again in a guest suite and—"

"Yes, I'll go. I don't want to go back to my house right now with everything that happened, and your family needs you. It's the safest compromise until I can get an alarm installed. Speaking of which, thank you for setting up a contractor." She'd cut him off because he didn't have to oversell the idea. Being with someone who had her back while she attended to her daughter's needs was exactly what she needed right now. If Cash was willing to be that person…even better.

A small part of her enjoyed being with a capable adult male for a change. The O'Connors seemed to have quite a few of them. By the end of her relationship with Jamison, she'd felt more like his caregiver than his life partner, and he'd become incredibly needy. It had come at a price of neglecting herself and her needs. She would never do that again in any relationship.

"The main house it is." Cash smiled, turned the key in the ignition and started his vehicle. Renee tried to ignore the part of her heart that wanted to convince her she could really like this man. Any relationship besides the new one she had with Abby was more than enough to handle even though her heart wanted to argue there was room for more.

A COUPLE OF steps inside the massive entryway to the main house, a noise sounded from down the hallway. Cash turned to Renee who was standing close behind him. Her arms literally felt like they might fall off at this point, but she couldn't put Abby down, either.

"That sound came from my mother's library. I want her to hear the news about Ruth Hubert from me. Are you okay with meeting my mother now? Because I can take you to the guest room first if you're not ready." Cash was sweet to consider her feelings.

"I'm fine, actually. I'd like to meet your mother very much. In fact, once this is all over, I'd like to get some parenting advice from her considering what an amazing job she's done with the sons I've met so far."

His genuine smile spread warmth through her chest and a desire to stand close enough to be in his sun.

She followed him to the opened double doors, where he knocked. "I'm sorry to interrupt you—"

"Don't be silly. Come on in. I could use the company." Margaret O'Connor had the kind of gentle but firm voice that took Renee back to third grade in Mrs. Malone's class. Renee smiled at the memory of her favorite teacher.

"I have a friend with me." The casual reference shouldn't cause disappointment. She mentally shook it off, figuring she was lucky to call an O'Connor a friend.

"The more, the merrier." Even though Renee didn't know Cash's mother, the words sounded like they were spoken with a forced cheeriness and she completely understood why.

One step inside the library halted Renee in her tracks. First of all, the floor-to-ceiling bookshelves were delicate and impressive. The room had endless layers of patterns and brass accents. Even the ceiling had a bronzed hue and a pattern that mirrored the rug. A granite frame and mantel flanked the fireplace on the opposite wall from the French doors. A deep orange sofa with leather club chairs made up the seating area. A pale blue ottoman anchored the room with a rug covering the floor beneath it. There were so many books it would be impossible to count them all. She took note of stacks of mysteries and true-crime novels.

The impressionist painting over the fireplace looked familiar and Renee was struck by just how wealthy a family the O'Connors were. Neither Cash nor Colton came off like they'd been born with silver spoons in their mouths. In fact, they were two of the most down-to-earth people she'd ever met.

"This is Renee Smith and her daughter, Abby," Cash said to his mother, who sat straighter as Renee walked toward her.

"Pleased to meet you," Mrs. O'Connor said in that genuine tone that brought Renee back to one of the few bright spots of her childhood. "Do you have time to sit for a minute?"

"Yes, ma'am—"

"Please, call me Margaret," she said with gray eyes that twinkled.

"It's a pleasure to meet you, Margaret." Renee took a seat as offered, grateful to get off her feet.

Margaret's smile widened when she looked at Abby, another thing that made Renee's heart swell.

"Your daughter sure is beautiful," Margaret said.

"Thank you." Renee couldn't help but beam at the compliment as she looked at her sleeping angel. "I'm so sorry about your husband."

Margaret looked up with the saddest eyes and nodded.

"May I hold her?" If it had been anyone else asking, the answer would have been a hard no. Margaret had the kind of gentle and elegant demeanor that put people at ease around her. Renee leaned toward her newfound friend and handed her daughter toward open arms.

Margaret's entire face lit up as she cradled Abby against her chest. Renee was beginning to see the magic of babies. She herself was pretty spellbound by the little angel and figured she could sit and hold that little girl for hours and completely lose track of time. Renee had never been much of a couch potato. She always liked to be up doing something, whether it was organizing a pantry or closet or trying—and mostly failing—to figure out how to craft.

Cash took a seat across the ottoman from

Renee. She glanced at him and her heart took another shot seeing the look on his face while he watched his mother hold a little girl. It occurred to Renee that he was about to deliver news about the attempted abduction. Abby was around the same age as his sister, Caroline, when she'd been taken from the family.

He didn't seem in a hurry to open that old wound. His cell buzzed in his pocket as Renee leaned back in the chair, grateful her arms were getting a break. She'd never met a person she trusted so immediately or so completely. Instead of being strange, it felt like the most natural thing.

"Excuse me," Cash said to the two of them. His gaze lingered when it met Renee's. She caught a worried look as it passed over his features. Margaret was too wrapped up to notice much else besides the miracle in her arms.

He walked into the hallway and his voice lowered to a hum. Renee couldn't make out what he was saying.

"I'm new to motherhood," Renee said to Margaret as she bit back a yawn. "I've met two of your sons so far and am so impressed with the amazing men they are. Any and all parenting advice is appreciated."

"The only thing a child really needs is love," Margaret said without hesitation. Those words shouldn't make tears threaten and yet they did. Unconditional love wasn't something Renee had a whole lot of experience with and her relationship with Jamison had caused her to doubt her ability to love or be loved by anyone. Abby was an exception as Renee knew a child would be. Rather than become angry at her parents for their self-involvement above all else, she felt sorry for them. Because they'd missed out on the greatest joy in Renee's life to date. Becoming a parent filled a longing from a place deep inside her. A place her parents had never reached with her. Or at least that's how it had felt.

Even when she'd been sick as a young child, they'd told her to stay inside her room. They would turn off her light and she was lucky if they remembered to check on her before they went to bed. Renee had come to accept her parents' lack of interest in her as normal behavior since it was all she'd ever known. She couldn't imagine doing the same now that she'd become a mother.

The family business had kept her parents up late hours arguing about money and dealing with all the paperwork that came with owning a small business. It was one of many reasons she'd considered early on that had led to her decision to work for someone else.

At five thirty every day, she was done with her job. Any web updates that needed to be made after that had to wait until morning. Once she left the building, she was off. She rarely had to work overtime or on a weekend. Although, she'd thrown herself into work and school to get where she was. When she worked overtime, it was her call.

The O'Connors seemed to be the exception to pretty much every rule. They obviously prioritized family over business and yet they ran one of the most successful cattle ranches. They had more money than they could spend, but it didn't seem to rule their lives.

Renee bit back another yawn as Cash stepped inside the room. With deep grooves in his forehead and a gaze that searched first for his mother and then for Renee, his expression was that of someone who was about to deliver more bad news.

Chapter Twelve

On instinct, Renee sat straighter as though a rigid spine would prepare her for any blow that came next.

Margaret was so busy being enthralled with Abby that she barely glanced up at her son. But when she did, she locked on to his gaze. "What's wrong?"

Cash reclaimed his seat. "Ruth Hubert was found murdered in her garden a few hours ago." That much, Renee already knew.

"Oh." With several sons who worked in law enforcement, Renee figured there wasn't much that shocked Margaret. "That's terrible news."

"Did you know her very well?" Cash asked his mother.

"Not really. I knew of her, but she mostly kept to herself. Our neighborhood committee has reached out to her several times over the years to see if she'd like to get involved in civic activities but she was never interested. She kept to herself mostly." A delicate eyebrow arched. "Why?"

"Deputies are going through her computer and phone records. They found links to a person who is widely suspected to be an officer in a trafficking ring that has been running for years."

"How far back does it go?" Margaret's interest seemed very peaked now.

"Decades." That one word seemed to let the air out of Margaret's lungs. She seemed to catch herself, as if her mood might impact Abby, and she straightened her chin and took in a breath after a quick glance at the baby in her arms.

"Does this link her to Caroline?" There was so much bravery in the steadiness of her voice in that question.

Cash heaved a sigh. "It might."

"Oh."

Renee's mind immediately snapped to Abby. Before she could open her mouth to speak, he nodded.

"There was an attempt to kidnap Abby," he said to his mother. "And Colton is investigating any possible links between the two cases."

"Kipp McGee." Renee said her lawyer's name practically under her breath.

Margaret looked confused. "Who?"

"He was the adoption lawyer for Renee,"

Cash supplied, his voice a study in calm. He had to have a million emotions drilling through him right now, too. There might be a break in his sister's case, on top of the fact he'd lost his father who was clearly a man Cash loved and respected.

Margaret's gaze flew to Renee. "I'm so sorry this happened to you and Abby." The sincerity in her words brought on more of those inconvenient emotions. *Acceptance* was another foreign word to Renee and yet it practically vibrated from Margaret.

"Thank you. It's been a difficult few days in a new city," Renee said. Even the quick burst of adrenaline that came with hearing the news couldn't stop her exhaustion from wearing thin.

"I can imagine," Margaret said with a look of solidarity. An invisible tether linked them and for the second time, Renee didn't feel alone. "You haven't slept much, have you?"

"To be honest, I'm afraid to do more than close my eyes for a few minutes. I'm scared that I'll wake and she'll be gone." A rogue tear escaped and slid down Renee's cheek.

Margaret's gray eyes widened before she nodded understanding. "Would you like to take her back?"

"Part of me wants to. But the other part knows

that I can trust you and my arms need a break," she admitted. "Unless you're tired."

"I could hold this angel all day." Margaret's words were soothing and there was so much sincerity in her eyes Renee didn't doubt the woman for a second.

"I brought them here to stay in the main house in the guest suite if that's all right with you," Cash said to his mother.

"What a great idea. Stay as long as you like." Margaret smiled through what must be difficult news to hear about her own case. This might be the first real break law enforcement had had. "Would you like to be shown to your room? We can set up a bassinet in the guest suite and Abby can sleep right next to your bed."

"If it's all right with you, I'd like to stay right here." The oversized club chair was the perfect size to curl up in and there was something so very comforting about being near Margaret. It was like Renee could finally let out the breath that she felt as though she'd been holding her entire life. The first time she'd experienced it had been with Cash.

"Make yourself at home. I'm more than happy to sit here awhile with your angel." Margaret's tone combined with the smile on her face said she meant every word. She started a low hum to one of Renee's favorite lullabies. Abby seemed perfectly content to stay put, so Renee slipped her shoes off and curled up in the chair.

Cash walked over, bringing a light blanket with him. He placed it over Renee with so much care tears pricked the backs of her eyes. She told herself that she was just running on empty and that was the reason for the emotion, but it was so much more than that. He was exactly the type of guy she could really fall for if she could take that step. She couldn't. Her past would always creep in, telling her she couldn't really trust anyone. She hugged the throw pillow and rested her head on the arm of the chair.

The next thing she knew, she was out.

CASH DIMMED THE lights in the library, trying to ignore how full his heart was at the scene of his mother holding Abby while Renee slept.

"Can I get anything for you?" he asked his mother quietly.

"Tea would be nice." The news about the investigation must have hit her hard but in true Margaret O'Connor form, she kept a handle on her emotions. Seeing her sitting there holding a six-month-old girl like she was the biggest prize hit him in a place very deep.

"I'm on it." He needed to step out of the room anyway before he lost all objectivity when it came to Renee's case. Or, if he was being honest, Renee.

Walking down the hallway toward the kitchen, he thought about all the times he'd heard about love at first sight but didn't believe it. Sexual chemistry? There was no doubt about that. Sexual chemistry was instant and there was plenty of that between him and Renee. He'd convinced himself that love at first sight was equivalent to a Bigfoot sighting. Lots of interesting characters claimed to have seen one over the years but always fell short when it came to producing evidence.

Whatever was going on between the two of them, he felt that lightning bolt hit square in his chest the minute he laid eyes on Renee. The feeling was different than anything he'd experienced before. He'd leave it at that.

The tea was in the exact same spot in the pantry as he remembered. He and his brothers had made it for their mother during holidays and special occasions. Her favorite black tea was there alongside a few he didn't recognize.

Heating water on the stove was old-fashioned and took more time, but he was feeling nostalgic today and, besides, he wanted a little extra time before going back to the library. The possibility that the person responsible for his sister's kidnapping could have been right underneath their noses his entire life sat like a hot poker in his stomach.

He leaned over the granite island and gripped his mother's favorite teacup. Realizing how delicate it was, he loosened his hold.

Ms. Hubert moved to the area roughly six months before Caroline's kidnapping. The MO was identical and yet no similar kidnappings had taken place in Katy Gulch in between. It felt possible the two kidnapping cases were linked. Improbable, but possible. What would the connection be? Two kidnapping cases decades apart?

Caroline and Abby were the same age at the time of the incidents. The heat brought on by Caroline's kidnapping back in the day might've caused the operation to shut down here in Katy Gulch. Maybe Ms. Hubert felt it was safe again to shop in her own backyard. Or, it was possible Abby fit the needs of someone willing to pay dearly for a child who looked like her. The elderly woman might not be the one calling the shots.

A burst of hope that his sister could somehow still be alive after all these years struck. Going down that road again—the one that made him believe he could find her for his parents—reopened a deep well of pain. Going there again was like walking into a fire without any gear.

Cash decided he needed to know everything there was to know about Ruth Hubert. He'd start there and see where the trail led him. His thoughts shifted to his brother Colton, who would be on the exact same track. Then there was Garrett. There was so much Garrett didn't know about here at home that he needed to be brought up to speed on.

Firing off a group text to his brothers, sans Garrett, Cash let them know the MIA status of their rogue sibling.

A few texts came back almost immediately. *Figures,* one of his brothers said. *Sounds about right,* came back from another. *What did you expect,* still another said. Colton was the only one who didn't respond, and he'd already been updated.

Any ideas on how we can find him? Cash asked.

The responses came quickly. They were all some version of *we'll see what we can do.* The teapot on the stove shrieked. Cash poured hot water over the tea bag and turned off the stove. Pocketing his phone, he brought the tea to his mother.

He set it down on the tray in front of her. Renee was asleep in the chair and his mother spoke quietly to a sleeping Abby. There was something a little too right about this whole scenario.

But he was also reminded of the circumstances that brought Renee to his family home. Then there was the loss of his father and a deep well of grief that had yet to fully surface.

"I never thought much about Ms. Hubert." His mother looked up at him. "She was so quiet. Folks whispered about her living all alone on the outskirts of town on enough land to grow pretty much anything she wanted, legal or not. She had visitors, folks said, so she'd be all right. People worried about her living out there all alone. And so did I. All this time she might've been the one..." His mother stopped herself before adding, "She might have been in plain sight all this time."

"I'd hate for you to be disappointed again," he said after carefully choosing his words. The last thing he wanted was to give his mother false hope. It had already stirred in his chest and was written all over her face.

"Your sister was a beautiful baby." She beamed down at Abby. "All of you were."

"She would be thirty-six now." His comment was met with a wistful smile.

"That's right." Her expression took a turn. "Do all your brothers know about your father yet?"

"Everyone but Garrett. We're trying to track

him down." He held back his opinion about his irresponsible and hotheaded younger brother. Cash had always been the eldest sibling despite his sister's age. With her gone, he'd stepped into the role.

"Oh. Any idea where he might be?" His mother's eyebrow shot up but she didn't look surprised. She seemed to accept that Garrett would drift in and out as he pleased.

"We checked his last job. He didn't exactly leave on good terms."

"He should never have worked for that family anyway. They've been branding our cattle and poaching from us for longer than I care to remember." His mother didn't normally talk badly about others. She'd always been the quiet type, preferring her library and her books to parties and gossip. The events she hosted usually benefited a charity and she played hostess in order to raise money, not out of a need to be the center of attention. She'd done a lot of good in the world. She deserved answers to her greatest personal misfortune—answers that investigators weren't able to give her and answers that neither Colton nor Cash had been able to provide.

She wouldn't see it this way, but it was impossible not to feel like he was letting her down in some way by not finding out what had happened to Caroline. Now that Pops was gone, she would need her family around even more.

Cash needed to think through his role on the ranch, which would be more than helping out in a pinch and with the busy season.

"Your father always wanted his sons to take over the ranch when they were ready." Her words hit him to the core.

"I have a career." Not only did he have a career, but he had one that he loved. Texas, this land, would always be part of his soul but his heart was in law enforcement. With the renewed possibility that they might have stumbled onto a lead in his sister's case, his blood was pumping again.

"Yes, you do. I didn't mean to make you feel guilty." She didn't give him a lecture and it occurred to him that she was planting a seed more than anything else. With their father gone, the family would need to have a meeting about how best to handle family business moving forward. Hard discussions needed to be had. There was no way Colton would desert his job as sheriff. Cash was certain about it. Other than Riggs, Garrett had the most experience working a cattle ranch, but could he be trusted to stick around? And, honestly, could he be trusted at all? Dawson was also a US marshal and he helped on the ranch as much as he could, much like the others, same as Blake who worked as a cop in Houston.

"Am I wrong to admit that I haven't given much thought to my role here on the ranch should anything ever happen to Pops?"

"No, you're not. No one saw this coming. Not me. Not your father. His doctor certainly thought he had more time." As far as young marriages went, she and Pops had beaten the odds. They'd met in high school and been sweethearts ever since. He'd opted to go straight to work for his family's ranch while she'd gone to University of Texas at Austin. Her parents hadn't thought Pops would be a suitable candidate for marrying their daughter since he hadn't gone to college. They'd told her that he might come from money, but she'd get bored of him because all he'd ever be able to talk about was cattle. Her father had refused to give his blessing for a marriage.

When Mother had told Pops, he'd cautioned her to think long and hard about her choices. Being cut off from family wasn't something he could have ever considered. Family had meant everything to Pops and it had to Mother, too. Pops had known deep down that she would have never been happy without her parents. He'd told her to take all the time she needed to think about it. That when a man met the woman who he was supposed to spend the rest of his life with, he could wait a few weeks or months for her to be certain of her choice to be with him.

He hadn't made it to his pickup truck before she'd asked, arms folded across her chest, if he was done with his speech. He'd said that he was. She'd told him to wait out front because she was going inside to get her bag.

Pops had always said waiting for her was the longest ten minutes of his life. When she'd returned, she'd told him that her parents might not approve but her heart did. She'd figured they'd come around once they saw how happy she was. The only regret she'd had was that she wouldn't finish college.

There was no desire that Pops didn't want his bride-to-be to fulfill. He'd refused to let her sacrifice her education for marriage. He'd said that he might not be able to bring her parents around, but he could ensure she got her degree.

So, she'd lived in a dorm Sunday night through Friday afternoon. Pops had driven to Austin every weekend to pick her up and bring her home to the ranch. Then he'd turned around and driven her back to campus. He'd made that trek for two and a half years without complaint.

As for the wedding? The preacher had been set to perform the ceremony at the ranch. Mother had invited her parents, but their seats had been empty with ten minutes to the wedding. Pops had overheard Gayle, Mother's best friend then and now, telling a friend that Margaret's mother had been heartbroken not to be able to witness her only daughter's wedding. It was the father who'd been holding out.

Pops had had everyone pile into the back of a couple of pickup trucks and had moved the entire ceremony to her parents' porch where his future mother-in-law could watch from the front window. Eventually, her father had come around and Pops had forgiven him. Because of Pops's big heart, Cash knew both sets of grandparents.

Cash would never consider himself a hopeless romantic by any means, but he loved hearing his parents' story. He looked at his mother when he said, "It's like a piece of us is gone without him and we will never be able to fill the hole."

"I know," she said with her characteristic warmth.

"The whole medical news came out of the blue," he admitted. She'd been right before. They would have to consider what to do next and especially if no one wanted to step up and help run the ranch. "I need a minute to think about my next steps."

"This place has been in your father's family four generations. There's so much history in these walls. I always felt privileged to be part of the O'Connor legacy." She looked him straight in the eyes. "Your father wanted to be here. It was his choice. He wanted the same for all of his children and that's the reason he never pressured any of you to work for him. He wouldn't want you to be miserable."

That was the thing, Cash didn't hate the idea of working more at KBR. He hadn't considered a life outside of law enforcement mostly because he figured Pops would live forever. There'd been no other possibility in his mind and especially since the man seemed in his prime physically. Cash had locked on to his career early and never looked back. "Maybe it's time to consider what's best for the family."

"What's best for each of you *is* best for the family."

While he understood what she was saying and appreciated her for it, he also realized that he didn't want the O'Connor family legacy to die with Pops. Cash and his brothers needed to talk about what their roles would be, if any of the others wanted one. Riggs was already on board. Yet, it wasn't fair to let all the responsibility fall on his shoulders. "I'll do my part to keep this place running."

There was also the question of what would happen to their mother if no one stepped up. KBR ran like a well-oiled machine, it could go on autopilot for the time being. Pops had hired an incredible team to take care of the cattle. He was one of the most respected men and employers in the state. Slim Jenkins was top when it came to his job as foreman. The man was like family. But Finn O'Connor was the captain who held the ship together. How long could it keep running smoothly without him?

Cash rubbed his forehead in an attempt to stem the headache trying to take seed. "First things first, I have to keep that kiddo and her mother safe. We need to lock away the bastard who tried to take this angel from her bed and then rip her from her mother's arms in a parking lot."

"The person came back a second time?" Mother sounded startled by the news.

"Yes."

She clucked her tongue and then looked down at Abby. "Sounds like someone wants this little girl very much."

"That's the way I'm looking at the situation. She has an ex I don't like. There was a creep from her office who can't be ignored. I'm following the evidence but this feels personal." And that most likely meant it was totally unrelated to Caroline's case because there was no connection between the families that he knew of.

"Why risk coming back?" Margaret O'Connor

had observation skills that would rival any good detective.

"The second attempt was made in the grocery store parking lot."

"In such a public place?" She balked.

"Exactly. It's been bothering me, too."

"Do we know who the birth parents are?" his mother asked.

"Not a clue. Colton interviewed her adoption lawyer a little while ago. We were at his office watching before we came here."

"And? How do you think it went?" She made a tsk-tsk noise. His mother could always be counted on to let people know how she really felt. She'd never been one to disguise her emotions, even when she put on a brave face.

"Poorly. He basically stopped the interview when Colton asked him to prove his whereabouts for the past forty-eight hours." Cash had taken note of McGee's body language and it didn't inspire confidence the man was innocent. Of course, the lawyer was already known to be shady, so that could very well be the reason. His nervousness might not have anything to do with Renee and Abby. He could, however, be connected to the Hubert murder. The lawyer might have believed the Hubert case was the reason he was being questioned. "He came across as squirrely to me."

"The guy sounds like a shady character." His mother had developed keen investigative skills over the past three and a half decades. He remembered the stacks of books in her library that she'd read and reread. Eventually, those gave way to mystery books.

"He's definitely someone to keep watch of, but that doesn't necessarily mean he was involved in the kidnapping attempts. He doesn't fit the description and trying to climb a ladder with his physical fitness level would be a challenge. The person who climbed in and out of Abby's window made the round trip quickly."

"Wouldn't Renee recognize her lawyer or anyone else she knew?" his mother asked.

"She couldn't see very well without her glasses on, so all she had was a general shape to go on. She didn't think it was him personally, which doesn't mean he's not involved and especially now that we found a link between him and Ms. Hubert."

"A man who hides behind his office wouldn't commit the crime himself." Her gaze narrowed. "No, he'd have henchmen do his bidding."

Cash sat for a long moment, contemplating his next question because it wasn't directly related to the case.

"Does it ever go away?" he finally summoned the courage to ask. No one ever spoke about

Caroline directly unless it was her birthday and then his mother would recount the precious few memories she had.

"Missing Caroline?" she asked.

"Yes. That ache. Does it ever get easier?" Even saying those words caused painful stabs in his chest.

"I'm afraid not, son."

"I'm sorry that happened to you and Pops," he said, wishing there was some way he could go back and fix the past to make it less painful for his parents.

"It happened to all of us."

Chapter Thirteen

"Abby." Renee sat bolt upright and searched the dark room for her daughter.

"She's right here." Margaret's soothing voice calmed Renee's nerves.

"Sorry." She blinked through blurry eyes, still half-asleep. It felt like the whole world was moving in slow motion, but that was probably just her. As her eyes adjusted to the light, she moved to the sofa next to Margaret.

Renee shook her head, trying to clear the fog.

"You tell me when you're ready for her." Margaret's kindness was water in a drought when it came to mothers.

"Is she okay?" Renee asked.

"She's an angel. We've been bonding."

"Does she need anything?" Renee could use a bathroom and a splash of cold water on her face to wake her up.

"She ate an hour ago and I changed her diaper after. I stayed right here in the library in case you woke. Cash did everything else and held her when my arms needed a break." Margaret smiled down at Abby. "She's a sweet baby."

"Thank you." Renee glanced around the dimly lit room. "Where is Cash?"

"In the office making a few calls. He didn't want to disturb you by making them in here. Should I call for him?"

"Maybe in a minute." There was something oddly comforting about being in this room with Cash's mother and Abby. It was obvious this woman would lay down her life before she'd allow anything bad to happen to either one of them, which struck Renee as remarkable considering they'd just met only a few hours ago. "How long was I asleep?"

"Probably not nearly long enough." Margaret chuckled. "About three hours."

"Your arms must be ready to fall off. I can—"

Margaret clucked her tongue. "I've had plenty of breaks with Cash around. Don't take her back until you're ready. Besides, it's been a really long time since I've held a little girl as lovely as Abby."

"She is a good baby, isn't she?"

"She really is." Considering Margaret's vast experience with little ones, Renee would take the compliment.

"Is there any chance I could trouble you for a cup of something warm?" Renee asked.

"Kitchen is down the hall. Help yourself to anything you want." Margaret nodded. "Or I could call Cash."

"No. That's okay. I don't want to be any trouble. I'll do my best not to get lost." She smiled but she also meant that very much. The main house was massive and beautiful from what she'd seen of it so far.

"I've lived here so long the place doesn't seem as big to me now as when I first moved in. This was my in-laws' place. I renovated once they handed over the reins in order to make it my own but I'd forgotten how overwhelming the place can be at first blush." She beamed back at Renee. "I hope you and Abby will make yourselves at home here. Cash is my oldest and he's not one to open up to people right away. That's always been my biggest worry with him. That he holds everything in." She sighed. "I'd like to tell you there's a point when you stop worrying about your children, but there isn't. Not until you see them happy." She paused a beat. "He's different when he's around you two. He could use a…friend." The way she said the last word made Renee think it was a substitute for the real one she wanted to say. There was so much warmth and love when Margaret spoke about her son. It was the same sunshine-on-a-warm-spring-day feeling she'd had when she first walked into their home. And, if she was being honest, when she'd first met Cash.

"I'm not sure what Abby and I would've done without your son." She felt her cheeks warm when she talked about him and was grateful for the dim lighting. Hopefully, his mother wouldn't see her physical reaction to talking about Cash.

"I couldn't be prouder of the man he's become." Margaret beamed. "Kitchen is down the hallway and to the left. I think you'll find everything you need there."

Renee thanked Margaret and headed out of the library. She pit-stopped at the bathroom and did a double take when she got a good look at herself in the mirror. Margaret had said to make herself at home, so Renee opened the medicine cabinet and located a few supplies for freshening up. It was the closest she could get to taking an actual shower. The toothbrush and toothpaste were like manna from heaven.

After washing her face and wrangling her curly waves into a ponytail, she headed toward the kitchen. The sound of fingers on a keyboard hit before she turned left. Someone was in the kitchen working. Cash had five brothers and there was plenty of hired help at the main house. This late, though, she figured she would most likely run into someone else in his family.

She didn't want to surprise whoever was in

the room and especially one of these men who were used to carrying weapons, so she cleared her throat as loudly as she could as she rounded the corner.

The minute she entered the room, Cash turned to face her and he stood up. Man, did her stomach perform a gymnastics routine the second their eyes met. Her body seemed to have a mind of its own when it came to the handsome lawman. Her brain was definitely out of its league when it came to controlling her physical response to him. The heart could want what it wanted all day long as far as she was concerned. Renee knew better than to let go of control like that despite how strong the urge was to do just that.

"Hey there," Cash said as his masculine voice conspired with her heart. "Did you get a good rest?"

"Surprisingly, yes." She tucked her hands inside her pockets for lack of something better to do with them. Knowing where to put her hands had never been a problem before now. She took in a deep breath and tried to remember why she came into the kitchen in the first place. "Tea." She didn't realize she'd said the word out loud until Cash nodded toward the counter.

"I'd be happy to get you a cup while I refill mine with something stronger."

"Oh, no. Don't go to any trouble—"

"I mean, it's no trouble. I was just about to get up." There was so much chemistry pinging between them that she thought she picked up on it in his voice, too. It was reassuring the attraction didn't seem to be one-sided.

"Okay. Well, if you're already getting yours." Her hands came out of her pockets and she shrugged in the most awkward of body movements. She knew exactly what she wanted— Cash. Her mind argued against the timing of an attraction as strong as this one. Logic tried to say that she felt this way only because he'd saved her and her baby…he was their rescuer or something like that.

Cash moved toward the counter and she was relieved when his back was turned to her so she could let out the breath she'd been holding. It was so much easier to think when those steel-gray eyes weren't locked on to hers.

Refocusing her attention on where he'd been sitting, she noticed he had a laptop and notepad on the massive oak table. "Find anything interesting?"

"Not really." As Cash brought over a steaming cup of tea that smelled like absolute heaven, his cell buzzed on the table next to the laptop.

Colton's name lit up the screen. Renee and Cash locked eyes for one second before he made a move to pick it up. The exchange between them, as electric as a hot-wired fence, sent more of that warmth sizzling through her. He set her cup down and answered.

"I'm putting you on speaker. Renee is here with me." The fact Cash seemed to need to immediately let his brother know who was in on the conversation with them made her wonder how much confidential information the brothers usually shared. Between the two of them, they had to be responsible for keeping many of the community's secrets, and she wondered how much of a burden that might be.

"Good." That one word from Colton sent a chill racing down her back because it meant he had news about her case.

She palmed her mug and rolled it around in her hands before taking a sip. The tea would provide much-needed calm.

Colton cleared his throat. "One of my deputies got an anonymous tip to pick up a young guy who works for the Pierson ranch. He was acting suspicious, so my deputy started digging around, asking questions. He told the guy our office would figure out if he'd done something wrong, lock him up and throw away the key. The kid got real nervous because he needs his job and room and board in the bunkhouse."

"Did this guy fit the general height and build of our window creeper?" Cash asked.

"He's a little smaller than the description she gave…"

Renee didn't want to point out that she didn't have her glasses on and so the guy's frame was more a blur. She'd been dead asleep and startled awake. She could've gotten this description wrong. It all happened so fast.

"But he confessed to being in the parking lot with two of his buddies. He said a man paid the trio a thousand dollars in cash to scare the mother."

Cash blew out a breath. "And you believed this kid?"

"By the time my deputy brought him in here the kid was almost inconsolable, especially when he found out what had happened a few hours before. He swears that he had no idea. He and his buddies thought the whole thing was some kind of twisted prank," Colton continued.

"So, these guys agreed to harass me and my daughter for a thousand dollars?" It was good to know what her life being turned upside down was worth to virtual strangers.

"The kid gave up his buddies' names and a deputy is on his way to pick them up to get their statements," Colton said.

"Do you believe him?" Cash's question was direct.

"Yes, I do. Obviously, I plan to follow wherever the evidence leads me but I think this kid is telling the truth." Colton didn't say how much this changed the course of the investigation. Cash had mentioned the crime seemed personal. It didn't get more personal than paying someone to…what?…scare her?

Renee took a sip of tea before taking a lap around the island. This place was the whole deal: farm sink, white granite countertops, double ovens. It looked like something out of a design magazine. And, yes, it did strike Renee as odd that she was noticing the decor when she'd just been thrown a curveball. Actually, she took that back. This was a fastball aimed right between her eyes.

"Why would someone do that?" She heard the words coming out of her mouth and revised. "Why would anyone pay another person to scare me."

Jamison came to mind. So did another name. The contractor from work. "Darion Figg."

"I had a chance to follow up with your boss earlier." Cash tapped his fingers on his mug.

Oh, darn. With everything going on the past few days she'd forgotten to give Rikki a heads-up about the call coming. "What did she say?"

"Mr. Figg seemed to develop a fixation on you and a couple of other female co-workers. Your IT department found incriminating pictures on his computer and he was fired not long after you complained about him. Once he lost his job, his girlfriend found out about what happened at work and left him."

"Seems like a pretty good reason to try to get back at me," she said. The creep deserved more than to be fired if he was snapping pictures of her and co-workers without their permission. She, for one, knew she'd never been asked. Another cold chill gripped her spine thinking about Darion. How many times had she turned around to suddenly find him standing behind her in the parking lot? In the beginning, she'd tried to be polite. She'd say, "Excuse me." Then, she'd walk away. He must've mistaken her politeness for interest because he'd pushed his body up against hers in the elevator, pinning her for a split second before she was able to shake off the shock of what had just happened and bring a knee up to his groin.

"The problem is that he's in county lockup on a drunk and disorderly charge. He got into a fight with a neighbor over where he parked his pickup," Colton said.

Cash shot a disappointed look her way. "That would make it impossible for him to be here."

Renee took another lap around the kitchen.

"Who did the kid say paid him? He must've met up with the guy if money changed hands."

Cash was right on track with what her next question was going to be.

"The kid said the whole transaction was handled in the men's room at the gas station. The money was slipped underneath a stall in a paper bag. Half up front. Half when the job was finished." Colton paused. "The kid flipped out when he realized how much trouble he was in. He's willing to cooperate but he doesn't know much about the guy who paid him. He was insistent that he was paid to scare her not to steal a child."

His statement explained why the suspects took off, and Renee found it reassuring they hadn't been out to steal Abby.

Who would hire someone to scare her? Who would pull a jerk move like that?

HEARING THIS, WATCHING Renee wear a path in his family's kitchen, Cash could see her tension building. She already had a white-knuckle grip on her mug of tea when the conversation started. Her stress levels seemed to be skyrocketing. Not an unusual reaction for someone who'd recently experienced one of the worst days of her life. But he wanted to do something to ease her stress. Since nothing came to mind, he asked Colton if there was anything else.

"That's what I have for now. I'll keep you

posted if anything changes," Colton said before saying goodbye and ending the call.

"Darion could've been behind what happened in the parking lot," she said as she approached the table with a whole heap of apprehension on her face.

"That's true. What would his motive be? Revenge?" Cash was just thinking out loud.

"It's weird to think someone could hate me that much. I did knock the wind out of him when he came on to me."

"Good for you. I hope the bastard thinks twice before he tries to force himself on another person. And I sure hope you nailed him where it counts." Cash would like five minutes alone with any person who tried to prey on someone they assumed was weaker than them.

"I doubt he'll look at women quite the same after the incident. He looked pretty shocked that I fought back, actually. He wasn't expecting a knee to the groin."

"Well, he deserved one." Cash picked up the pen on the pad of paper and twirled it around his fingers.

"My mind is flooded with possibilities. Darion could've hired someone from jail," she offered.

"A drunk like that isn't usually capable of arranging a money exchange. He wouldn't have been in contact with anyone on the outside if he was sleeping off a binge, so it would've been impossible for him to communicate." Cash was already running through possibilities in his mind.

With Renee standing so close to him, he could smell her floral scent. She smelled like spring flowers after a good rain. He was also aware when she shifted from frustration to need. It wasn't uncommon for someone who'd been through trauma to want proof of life.

When she locked gazes with him, her glittery blue eyes sent a shot straight to his heart. He was taking on fire being so close to her. He should remain partial and step away, despite the signals she was sending.

"Cash." Her warm honey tone wrapped around him.

"Yeah." He could hear the huskiness in his own voice when he spoke.

"Can you do me a favor?" Her body language wasn't difficult to read and yet he still wasn't prepared for the next couple of words that came out of those soft pink lips.

"Depends on what it is." There was a lot of ground her question could cover. Cash didn't make promises he couldn't keep. His word was his honor.

"Kiss me."

Chapter Fourteen

Cash took in a sharp breath, closed the distance between him and Renee in a couple of steps and leaned in.

She closed her eyes and leaned toward him. He knew exactly what he wanted…her. Was it smart? Was he crossing a line that couldn't be uncrossed if he finished what he'd started?

Granted, she'd never felt like a victim to him, no matter how much his protective instincts flared when she was around. The pull toward her was stronger than anything else he'd ever experienced. But cross that line and there was no going back. His professionalism was at stake in a career he'd worked his tail off to build.

"Cash." His name came out as barely a whisper.

He flexed and released his fingers because they itched to get lost in her hair. His mouth was so close to hers. Damn. He rested his forehead against her.

"Believe me when I say that I couldn't want to kiss you more than I do right now."

"But…"

"It would be a game changer for me." He meant that on so many levels even though he couldn't articulate the reasons if he tried. On instinct, on a primal level, he realized Renee was different. She was intelligent and determined and beautiful on more levels than he could count.

"I can't afford game changers in my life right now. Not after my breakup with Jamison. I'm sorry," she said.

"My job is to protect you, not confuse you." Everything in Cash wanted to take that final step, consequences be damned. He didn't get to where he was today by giving in to impulses. He'd been calculating about his life choices and would be the same way if the right circumstances happened for him and Renee to move forward with what they both so obviously wanted in the moment.

Cash didn't do or give regrets.

"I'm pretty damn clear about what's good for me. Kissing you falls into that category. Doing anything else, anything more…not so much."

"Take a step down that slippery slope and we can't come back." One kiss wouldn't be enough with Renee. Where would that leave them? One great kiss followed by a helluva lot of nothing. Because it couldn't go anywhere in the middle of an investigation. Granted, it was his brother's investigation, but Cash was acting as consultant on this one and since he'd stepped in on the initial call, he was committed to seeing this through. The annoying voice in the back of his mind called him out as a liar. He'd never once brought a victim to the main house for protection no matter how personally responsible he felt for their safety. Cash knew himself. He had a tendency to go all in whether it meant family or work.

Was that part of the reason he'd shied away from relationships? He didn't have it in him to go all in with a woman?

Why the hell did his mind pick this moment to reveal that his heart had already fallen down that slippery slope he'd been talking about a few seconds ago.

"No." She paused for a thoughtful moment. "But we could hang on to each other while we brace for the fall."

Cash needed to refocus. He needed to force his thoughts away from those full pink lips of hers. He needed to think about something besides how silky her skin would feel if he reached his hand up. And he sure as hell needed to stop imagining what she might taste like because this close he figured it would be a mix of tea and peppermint, basically Christmas.

He brought his hands up to cup her face. Temptation was two inches away from his mouth and stood at five feet, seven inches tall. He could feel her pulse racing, the tempo matching his.

Cash's cell buzzed again, indicating a text had come in. Since it could be news about the case, he dropped his hands on a hard sigh. "Think we can talk about this...*us*...later?"

"Yeah." She was breathless when she spoke and a little satisfied smile quirked the corners of his mouth up. Renee Smith had one hell of an effect on him. It made him feel better than it should that she seemed to have the same reaction to him. Under any other circumstance, she was exactly the kind of person he'd want to get to know better. He envisioned them dating and...

Holy hell. His thoughts had a mind of their own when it came to Renee. They needed to stay in check. He reminded himself of the facts. She'd been through a lot. She was most likely just reaching out for comfort. It wouldn't have mattered who'd been standing there...

He couldn't sell himself on the last line because her reactions to him had been too real. No matter how much he tried to convince himself otherwise, whatever was going on between them was special. He'd be smart to keep a firm handle on his emotions.

It had been a really long time since he'd cared about someone *this* much, and he barely knew Renee Smith.

"Why are you smiling when I'm this…*frustrated?*"

"This is how I handle frustration." It was true.

She laughed and it broke the tension between them. Granted, it was sexual tension but that was the most intense he'd ever felt. Laughter was a good thing about now.

"What does your phone say?" She picked up her tea and took a sip. Immediately, she scrunched up her face. "Well, that went cold on me fast."

That comment really made him laugh. She locked gazes with him and broke into a wide smile when she picked up on the undercurrent.

"I'm just going to leave that comment alone and heat my tea." She made a show of looking for the microwave.

"That way." He pointed to the opposite end of the kitchen.

"This place is so big. I don't think I've ever been in a kitchen this large before and I was a waitress once."

Cash studied the screen and didn't respond.

He heard the microwave beeping and figured she'd found her way. A half-dozen bombs were exploding inside his head as he reread the message.

"Cash?" Renee studied him as she made a beeline toward him. "What is it? What's wrong?"

"It's the Hubert case. We found email ties to the Ludlow kidnapping ring. The feds have been gathering information about them and their involvement with bigger crime organizations. Basically, they are considered one of the biggest illegal adoption operations in the Southwest."

"She can't be connected to my case, can she?"

"It's possible. She might've paid the kids to scare you to throw us off the track," Cash stated.

"Or the person she reported to might have done it after the kidnapping attempt was messed up."

"True. Your crime has felt personal but that could just be what they want us to think. Like you said, throw us off the trail after botching the job." Cash had seen pretty much everything in his life as a marshal.

Renee gasped. "She might have been murdered to prove a point."

"Or to keep her quiet. Maybe whoever is really in charge thought she brought too much heat to the organization. Believe me when I say these operations run better than most Fortune

500 companies. They have to. There's so much more at stake than disappointing shareholders with earnings. These are live by the sword, die by the sword people. Literally."

"I know she's safe but hearing this makes me want to go check on Abby." Worry lines creased Renee's forehead.

"I'll go with you. My mother needs to hear the news." He bit back a curse.

"Your sister?"

"I don't want to get my mother's hopes up because there's no concrete evidence to link Ms. Hubert to Caroline despite the timing of her moving to town," he hedged. "My mother should hear this news from one of her sons and not through the grapevine or a news outlet."

"Small towns do breed a tight-knit community. It's one of the many reasons that I wanted to leave Dallas. I love my city, but it's grown so much that it can feel impersonal at times. Neighbors don't really know each other anymore and especially not in the suburbs where I lived."

"I can't imagine not knowing the people I lived around. Stacy has become like family as much as everyone who's worked here a long time. But then, my job reminds me we only know the face people show us. Doesn't mean it's who someone truly is." Cash picked up his cup of coffee. "Better head to the library now. Are you coming?"

"Yes, but I'll only stay if you want me to."

There was a lot he wanted from her. He'd settle for this. "My mother has been through a lot. And now with Pops—"

"Yes, of course. You probably want to be alone. This is family time." She sure knew how to backpedal. If she had on running shoes she'd probably be hitting the door about now.

"I was actually about to say that having you and Abby here is a bright spot in what has otherwise been an awful couple of days. I've never seen her hold a six-month-old girl before. My brother has sons and she loves them with all her heart. There's always been a special spark in her eyes when she looks at a little girl."

"Don't tell me stuff like that. Okay?" It was pure protective instinct causing her to speak up. The fact that Abby was welcomed by Margaret sent more of that warmth spiraling through her. She couldn't afford to let anyone else in right now.

Cash studied her before he responded. She'd expected him to get angry or demand a reason like Jamison would've. Instead, he crossed his arms over his chest and seemed to look right through her. "Mind if I ask why not?"

"Because right now getting my bearings on being a mother is my absolute first priority. It's all I have time for." Letting anyone else in her heart when it had just been so broken seemed like a suicide mission. She'd taken her time getting to know Jamison, at least she'd convinced herself that she knew him, and look how that had turned out. Her heart had been stomped on. And it should feel…it should feel a lot worse than it did. She'd convinced herself that she was having some kind of delayed reaction.

She'd been mad as hell at him when she'd found out about the affair. It had never gutted her in the way losing a man like Cash would.

Damn. Was that her real concern? Not that Cash couldn't care about her but that her feelings for him might run too deep? So deep that if he walked out one day her heart might not survive?

Cash's eyebrows drew together. He studied her for a long moment and he looked at her like he could see right through her. It should startle her. Instead, there was a comfort like she'd never known. Acceptance that she'd wished for her entire life.

Now, she realized, it was good that he didn't act on their mutual attraction no matter how much she'd wanted him to. Kissing him *would* be a game changer. She would leave it at that and back away from the thoughts in her mind telling her it was about time the game was changed.

"You're welcome to come back here and use the laptop. I'll be back in a few—"

She waved her hands in the air to stop him from finishing his sentence. Margaret O'Connor had been nothing but kind to Renee since she'd walked in the door. She trusted the woman enough with her daughter to fall asleep as well as leave the room once she woke. If Renee's presence could provide some small measure of comfort to the person who'd been so kind, so be it. "Never mind, Cash. I'd like to stay with you."

He probably had whiplash from her change in plans.

"She'd like that, Renee."

Instead of overthinking the offer, she turned and walked toward the library.

The sight of Margaret O'Connor holding Abby stirred more emotions. Renee had never felt so vulnerable to something so little or so emotional.

"She really is a good girl," Margaret cooed.

"Is she awake?" Renee performed a double take. Abby's eyes were wide open. Instead of being afraid of the stranger, she smiled and cooed right back. The grandmotherly image brought out a longing for something that Renee hadn't even realized had been missing. Abby had no grandparents. And with Renee's parents long gone and no other side of the family to count on, it was just going to be the two of them. The statement had never felt lonely until now, until the O'Connors, until Cash.

"She's been awake since you left. I think she sensed you were gone. She's comforted by you being here." Margaret's words made more of those hot tears prick the backs of Renee's eyes. She wanted more than anything for them to be true. "We've been keeping each other company, though. I figured you needed a minute. How's the tea?"

"Good," Renee answered quickly. Probably a little too quickly.

The astute woman's eyebrow lifted ever so slightly. Her gaze went to Cash and held. "You have something on your mind."

"Yes, ma'am."

"You are both welcome to sit down. And, as much as I've loved holding this little angel, she's ready for her mother." Margaret must've felt Renee's apprehension as she handed over a happy Abby.

Renee took a seat on the couch next to Margaret. It was easy to feel at home with the O'Connors and especially with her daughter in her arms.

Cash reclaimed his seat from earlier. "I got a text from Colton a few minutes ago. The investigation into Ms. Hubert's death is turning over a few stones and I don't want you to be caught off guard."

"The media will be back full force, asking questions. They'll figure out a way to get my cell number and hound me again." She looked at Renee with the most determination she'd seen. "They used to pay folks to give my number to them after Caroline was taken. That was back in the day when we had house phones and landlines. Finn and I couldn't leave the property for fear of being followed. I had my bumper tapped on the way to town once by a reporter. We figured it wasn't safe to go on the roads until everything died down. Of course, back then we thought they'd find her and bring her home. We endured the publicity because we thought it might help bring her back to us."

"I can't begin to understand what you went through. I'm so sorry." Renee patted Margaret's hand. Much to her surprise, the older woman gave a reassuring squeeze.

Margaret turned to her son. "What do they know so far?"

He leaned forward and filled his mother in. He spoke with so much compassion. The love and respect between him and his mother was big enough to fill the room.

"And now you fellas are thinking Caroline's case might be connected?" She seemed to already know the answer to her question but asked anyway.

"I just wanted to warn you of the possibility. You know how many twists and turns there can be in an investigation. Ms. Hubert's case spans a lot of years. No doubt, the media will make the connection and folks will be talking about Caroline again." Before he finished his sentence, his mother was nodding.

"Any kidnapping news that involved a child under the age of one caused her name to be brought up. You'd think it would bother me. I never minded, though. I figured it couldn't hurt to talk about her again. The nagging feeling that someone must've seen something that night never left me. The person might not have even realized they'd seen anything important. You hear about these stories of crimes being solved ten or twenty years after the fact because a witness pops up out of the blue not realizing the red sedan they'd witnessed driving away from some crime scene would lead investigators to the offender. That's always been the problem. Whoever took Caroline was able to blend right in."

Renee took note of the stack of true crime

books on the table next to her. There were stacks of mystery novels, too.

Margaret motioned toward a particularly large pile. "I can't even count the number of hours I've spent in here trying to train my brain first to think like a criminal and then a detective."

Cash's hands were folded together and there was so much reverence in his eyes. It clicked with Renee that he and several of his brothers went into law enforcement for their careers. She wondered how much of it had to do with the very real pain still present in Margaret's eyes.

It struck her just how much one event could alter the course of someone's life forever. If Abby's kidnapper had succeeded...

Renee couldn't continue with that train of thought.

Caroline's kidnapping had shaped this family. For Renee, her parents' car crash had altered her life in so many countless ways. While she'd closed herself off from the world, the O'Connors seemed to have used their tragedy to pull together and form even tighter bonds. Maybe that was the difference between growing up alone versus being in a large, loving close-knit family.

"I failed her—"

Margaret's voice broke. She shushed Cash when he tried to offer words of comfort. Those three words amounted to Renee's biggest fear. She'd felt that same helplessness when she woke the other night. The man in Abby's room couldn't possibly have been there only to scare Renee. She'd caught him red-handed picking up her daughter from the crib.

The cover-up might have been intended to throw them offtrack. The idea that Caroline's case could be related to Abby's all these years later was a terrible possibility.

"News will get out about Abby soon. I guess the comparisons are coming no matter how long it's been. I'm more worried about that to be honest." Margaret clucked her tongue in disapproval. "I want to find out what happened to my daughter, but I don't want to overshadow your investigation. It's no good if people get distracted."

"No, it isn't," Cash agreed. Those words scared Renee. She wouldn't be able to leave her daughter's side or sleep alone in a house again until the perp was caught.

Freaking out every time the doorbell rang or being too scared to go to the store sounded like living in a prison.

Margaret fell quiet for a long time. She looked tired, weary. The glow from holding Abby had faded.

The older woman pushed up to standing. "We

won't solve anything tonight. I'd probably better try to get some sleep." She turned to Renee. "Thank you for letting me hold your angel. She's a lucky little girl to have you as a mother. I hope you'll come to me with any questions you have. I'm not sure that I know much, but I'm happy to share what I've learned over the years."

"I will take you up on that. I'm grateful for any advice." Renee meant every word. She was rewarded with a warm smile.

"Cash, will you show her to her quarters?"

"Yes, ma'am." He stood and wrapped his mother in a hug. Another one of those rogue tears leaked from Renee's eyes. She ducked to cover it while she wiped it away. His mother had to know Renee already knew where her room was, so she took the suggestion as a sign Margaret wanted to be alone.

"Do you want me to take her?" he asked, nodding toward Abby.

"No, thanks." She needed her daughter to keep her arms busy. Especially because what they wanted was to reach out and touch Cash.

Chapter Fifteen

Renee reviewed the facts once she was settled in the comfortable guest room.

The mystery mover's identity had been revealed. He had a solid alibi as did his crew chief, Paul. They'd learned earlier that the lighter, a piece of evidence she'd hoped might lead to the perp, belonged to Paul.

Darion Figg was in jail, which didn't necessarily rule him out but made pulling off the crime more difficult. He had the perfect motive along with an equally perfect alibi. He had harassed other women at the office. The reason he'd been fired had to do with the pictures found on his work computer and wasn't necessarily the direct result of her complaint about him. Some of her other office mates had come forward, too. So, the trail of revenge should be longer than just Renee.

Kipp McGee was tied to a murdered woman who was linked to a kidnapping ring. Why give

Abby to Renee in the first place if he was only going to turn right around and take her back? She needed to think through why someone would do that. What would his reasoning be? Didn't he have to have a motive?

She looked up at Cash. "Something has been bothering me about Kipp McGee. Why give Abby to me only to take her back a month later? Why not cut out the middleman altogether if he had the baby in his care in the first place? He was the one who brought her to me."

Cash leaned back in the chair beside the bed. "For one, to throw people off the trail of who the baby was really going to. You hired him to do a job. He delivered. He collects his fee and makes you think he moved on."

"He's never been inside my new house. Didn't you say early on the perp seemed to know the layout?"

"Being from the area and having been in countless homes, it wouldn't be difficult for McGee to guess the layout." He made a good point.

"I know it wasn't him that first night, though. It sounds like you're saying he would've hired someone to…*do it* for him." She couldn't bear to say the words *take her*.

"Right," Cash agreed.

"So, someone botches the first attempt and

then tries to cover with the guys from the grocery store parking lot. And then an anonymous tip leads the investigation to him, but he can't give any details about the person who hired him. It doesn't make sense to me," she said. "Why would someone go to all that trouble?"

"To change the motive. To distract investigators and lead them down a different path," he stated.

"Jamison is missing and so is Yolanda," she reminded him.

"The investigation is all over the place right now, which could indicate the perp is an amateur. He might've started to take your child and then panicked when you caught him. It was maybe supposed to be a quick in-and-out job. But you ruined that so he had to hire someone to throw us off." Cash rubbed the scruff on his chin, a habit she'd noticed him doing when he was stressed.

"And then there's Darion." She crossed her arms over her chest and hugged them. It was strange thinking about who might have a grudge against her.

"Getting drunk and being locked up gives him an airtight alibi," Cash said.

"For both attempts."

"He couldn't have known the first attempt

would fail and I seriously doubt he could pull off the second one from jail," Cash reasoned.

"It sounds safe to erase him from the suspect list then." At least they were able to cross a couple of names off the list so far.

Cash nodded. "Unless new information comes up to change our minds, we can go ahead and rule him out for now."

"You said something early on that has stuck in my mind ever since. You stated that the crime seemed personal because of the second attempt happening so soon. Have you changed your opinion?"

"My personal opinion? No." Cash's cell buzzed. He checked the screen and then gave her a look that sent her stress levels soaring before picking it up. The look was becoming familiar and meant Colton had another message.

Cash studied the screen. "There were no prints on the ladder."

"Wouldn't there be *someone's* prints on there?" Someone had to have touched it at some point. Right?

"It was wiped clean. Considering the perp took off after being interrupted, he had to have wiped the ladder beforehand. And it also means he wore gloves so we're not likely to get any viable prints at your house, either." He issued a sharp sigh. "There's something else. Yolanda

Tran answered Colton's call. She said that she and Jamison are on a babymoon and that he's been with her since the doctor's appointment."

"Does that mean he's ruled out?" A part of her wished it was true. She didn't want someone she'd once cared about and trusted to be responsible for one of the most horrendous acts against her.

Cash looked up from his phone. "I'm never thrilled when a person's alibi hinges on someone else who has a lot to lose. Plus, their story seems to be changing from a doctor's appointment to a babymoon."

"Paul's mother might have a lot to lose, right?" It clicked why. It was probably common for a person to lie, cheat or steal to protect someone they loved. The reasoning made perfect sense and yet it all still had a huge ick factor. Renee had always been one to follow the rules. Then again, she'd never been in a situation where she'd had to protect someone she loved. She glanced over at Abby's crib. Her protective instincts were already so strong. But what example would she set for her daughter if Renee was willing to do anything at all costs to cover for her. Protecting and covering were two different things in Renee's book. Clearly, not everyone shared her morals.

"Right. Besides, he could've tricked her into

thinking he was home when he wasn't." What he was saying made perfect sense.

"Yolanda has a lot to lose if Jamison goes to jail right before she gives birth to their child."

"What else can you tell me about your ex, though?" he asked.

"Like?" Renee would like to forget as much about him as she could, but this might be important to the investigation. Again, it should seem strange sharing so many personal details with him. Instead, it was like talking to someone she'd known her whole life.

"What were his habits? How did he deal with stress?"

"He changed a lot over the years. I mean, when we first got together, he could be a little possessive. I tried to break up with him over it but he convinced me to stick around. He was great in the early days. He once drove two hours round trip to put a single flower on my car with a note telling me to have a great day. But it grew from there and started to worry me that he was getting too attached, too soon. When I put my foot down about him showing up unannounced at the restaurant where I worked, he stopped." Or so she'd thought, until now. It was highly possible that he'd been keeping track of her over the years without telling her.

"From the sounds of it, he pursued you pretty hard."

"Looking back, I guess that's true. He definitely had to convince me to go out with him in the first place," she said.

"You weren't interested in him?" An eyebrow arched.

"Not him. Not anyone. I'd lost my parents the year before we started dating and their relationship had left a sour taste in my mouth. I was working at a restaurant to pay for classes at my community college. The business my parents owned was in bad financial shape. It's part of the reason they fought all the time. I'd been living at home, working my way through school when the accident happened."

"I'm sorry for your loss." Those words soothed her soul. Despite not having a great relationship with her parents, she was still sad they were gone.

"Thank you. While they were alive, there was still a chance to make things right. You know?"

He nodded his understanding and she appreciated his compassion, but how could he know what it was like to come from a broken family?

"Our home was foreclosed on and I had to find a place to live. I rented this tiny apartment over an older couple's garage. I had no way to bring furniture. I couldn't afford to buy anything, so I slept on a pile of blankets on the floor. I kept working despite everything I was going through. I managed to stay in class, barely able to afford to keep going. But I did and I got an associate degree and tech certification, so now I can support myself and my daughter."

"Wow." He sat back and blinked at her like she'd just dropped a bomb in his lap. "I knew you were strong and capable when I first interviewed you but this…most people would buckle under those circumstances, not fight."

It was strange to hear from an outsider's perspective considering she'd never talked about her past with anyone. Even Jamison seemed content to take her at face value when she said that she and her parents weren't close, but that she'd loved them. He'd never once seemed amazed by what she was able to accomplish, but then she'd never really gone into much detail, either. Looking into Cash's eyes now, his admiration was almost overwhelming. "I did what I had to in order to survive. Anyone in my position would do the same."

She tried to shrug off his compliment.

"I'd say you're doing a helluva lot better than surviving. Not many people could pick up the pieces of their life and thrive, considering the obstacles life threw at you early on."

She was surprised she wanted to tell Cash

about her past. She was used to downplaying or hiding it.

"I never talk about the past. Part of me thinks I've bottled all my emotions up for so long that it's just become the elephant in the room of every friendship, every relationship." Renee was surprised at how much she wanted to open up to a stranger. Except that Cash O'Connor didn't exactly fit into that category. There was a spark with him that she'd never felt before with another man. The connection between them couldn't be faked. And she should be embarrassed that he'd rejected her advance before but she wasn't. The fact he'd wanted her as much as she wanted him—well, almost—comforted her. She was on the right track. He felt the chemistry between them as much as she did. And he made it seem like it was taking all of his self-control to keep their relationship platonic.

"It's easy to do. Tuck an emotion into a box and stuff it down deep." He stared at the wall when he spoke. As wonderful of a mother as Margaret had to have been, losing her firstborn in the way she had would've altered the rest of her life.

"The work you do is dangerous. Does that ever bother you?" She wanted to know more about his decision to go into law enforcement versus the family business.

"There's not much more danger than ranching."

"How?" She was genuinely curious. She'd talked enough about herself and wanted to know more about Cash.

"Poachers, for one. Cattle rustlers are another serious threat. Wild animals have taken down a few men over the years. Wild hogs are nasty and dangerous. Human error while running equipment can be deadly, and is one of the biggest killers. And then there's Mother Nature herself."

"Wow. I had no idea. The biggest threat in the suburb where I used to live was traffic." Dallas traffic was a force to be reckoned with for sure.

"I still have a whole helluva lot of respect for what you've been able to accomplish despite tough beginnings." He managed to cycle the conversation back around to her.

"You managed to make something of yourself despite growing up in a place like this." She was still in awe of the O'Connor family home. It was something to behold.

"Are you saying that I could've ended up a trust fund baby? Because I doubt that would float on a hard-working cattle ranch like KBR." He laughed and it broke some of the intensity of the conversation. She figured it was part defense mechanism to laugh when the conversation turned serious. She'd been guilty of that herself, which made it easier to recognize in someone else.

The break in tension was a welcome reprieve. It also made her think of normal things, like taking a shower.

"Any chance I can grab a shower while she's sleeping?"

His smile was devastating. He shook his head. "Probably not a good idea to put the image of you naked in my...never mind." He nodded toward the en suite bathroom. "I already had your clothes brought to the main house and the others have been washed. You should find them in there."

Being with Cash, with someone who thought about her needs, stirred more of those falling-into-the-deep-end feelings in her chest. She took in a breath, smiled to herself and walked into the bathroom.

"You'll be okay with her if she wakes?" Renee stopped at the door. He didn't want to notice the soft curve of her hip, so he adjusted his focus.

"Did okay with twin nephews at this age. I think I can handle one." Technically, he'd been alone with them only once. This wasn't the time to discuss his qualifications, or lack thereof. As close as he was to Colton and all of his brothers save for Garrett, Cash had always been married to his work. If Abby stirred, he could figure out a way to handle the situation while Renee showered. She seemed to trust him and quietly closed the bathroom door behind her.

Cash opened the laptop he'd brought with him from the kitchen, which pulled up one of his favorite family pictures. It was the summer before senior year. Cash and his brothers had been working the ranch and, for reasons he couldn't pinpoint now, he and Garrett had gotten into an argument. The day had been a scorcher. The temps had topped off at one hundred and seven for the third day in a row. All six boys had been working the ranch since four o'clock, his father's usual wake-up time. It was the time of year in Texas when the weather never cooled off.

So, it was probably teenage hormones baking in a hot sun all day that had him and Garrett on edge with each other. Garrett had popped his mouth off about something or other and Cash had stomped over and gotten in his brother's face. Wrong move. As an adult, he'd learned to reason his way out of most situations. Foolish pride had him challenging Garrett, poking the angry bear.

Garrett had always been a hothead, so it hadn't been difficult to get him riled up. Cash had probably just needed to blow off some steam. Garrett had thrown the first punch. The two of them had ended up on the ground in a wrestling match. Until their mother had caught wind of what was happening.

She hadn't raise her voice. They'd had no idea she was even there until the bucket of ice-cold water doused them.

Two people had never jumped up so fast in their lives. Both ready to fight because they'd had no idea they'd be staring Margaret O'Connor in the face. Even then, she'd been a tiny storm best left untouched. The rest of his brothers had stood in a semicircle, snickering, which had gotten Cash and Garrett in even more trouble because they'd both started cracking up. Their mother hadn't seen the humor in her sons getting into a fistfight.

Pops had heard the commotion from the barn. Next thing Cash knew he'd been staring down both of his parents. Pops had asked what had happened.

Garrett had started by saying, "Well, sir. My brother here is a donkey's backside."

At those words, Cash had lost it. Just when he'd expected to be reamed out, Pops had laughed, too. That'd made their mother crack up. She'd walked to him and Garrett and pulled them both into a hug. Her dress had been soaked. Pops had picked her up and pretended he was about to toss her into the pond. She'd been as calm as she could be when she'd dared him to do it.

Even Pops had known not to cross his wife. She was five feet, five inches of pure dynamite. Slim Jenkins had watched the scene unfold. He'd told everyone to squeeze in for a picture. All of the boys had groaned. But they'd done it. The picture was of Pops carrying his wife and their boys flanking them, two of whom were soaked to the bone in pond water.

Everyone had a silly smile plastered on their face. All of which were the real deal unlike those Christmas card pictures their mother had liked to force on them. At least she hadn't insisted they all wear the same sweater. It could've been a lot worse.

But this was Cash's all-time favorite family pic. It was messy. The boys were precocious. Their parents loved the family no matter what, dirty pond water and all.

This was the real O'Connor family. Despite Garrett's current shortcomings, he needed to know what was going on. Pops had never wanted a real funeral. He'd be angry that everyone was so sad when there was work to get done.

No doubt, Margaret O'Connor would respect her husband's wishes. There would be a small ceremony, a remembrance, a celebration of his life. A few tears slipped out at the thought of Pops never walking through the back door again, sweaty from a hard day's work and still dressed in a long-sleeve button-down shirt. Although most cattle ranchers used pickup trucks to herd cattle nowadays, Pops considered himself a renaissance man. He rode his horse every day to check fences to see if any part needed repair. Most people would be surprised at just how much of a cattleman's life was spent doing paperwork and checking fences to ensure the safety of their livestock.

Wiping blurry eyes, Cash zeroed in on his email. With his cell phone almost constantly being available, he hadn't thought about sending his brother an email. Since no one else had come up with any better ideas, Cash pulled up their last exchange. He checked the date. It had been three years ago. His brother wasn't the type to have a social media account, so this was his best bet for the time being.

But what should he say over email? He didn't want to puke the news out without preparing Garrett for what was coming. He also needed the note to sound urgent enough to get his brother's attention.

Garrett,
I realize we've been out of touch. You're needed at home. There's serious news. Call or come home.
Your brother,
Cash

It wasn't Shakespeare, but it got the point across. He added his cell number under his name in case Garrett wanted to reach out.

Cash took a deep breath and hit Send. There was no good time to deliver bad news, and he hated that Garrett didn't already know.

Rubbing his temples, he tried to stave off one helluva headache. The shower water was on full force in the adjacent bathroom. He could hear it even through the door. And, yes, his thoughts immediately went to Renee standing naked in the shower. But he managed to refocus.

Staring at a computer screen wasn't helping the throb above his eyes, and besides, his mother had always repeated the phrase about a watched pot never boiling. As he lowered the screen, a message popped up.

It was from Garrett.

Lost my cell. On my way home.

Chapter Sixteen

Cash couldn't sleep if he tried. He'd gone days without shut-eye before while working a case and this one was shaping up to be no exception. Rather than fight it or dread it, he settled in as he heard the water turn off in the adjacent room.

He texted his brothers to let them know Garrett was on his way home. Then he messaged their mother. She needed to know her son was coming.

Unless they were missing something, there were three suspects left in Renee's case: McGee, Jamison and Yolanda.

The lawyer reopened old wounds with his connection to another town resident. A feeling of dread that Ms. Hubert could be linked to his sister's case was growing, niggling away at the back of his mind. The reality of losing his father was also starting to sink in. It had been one helluva couple of days since meeting Renee.

Much of Cash's life was being turned upside

down and there was still a sense of rightness in the world with Renee and Abby in the picture.

Just as he thought about Renee, she came walking out of the bathroom. His heart took another dive. Renee was beautiful, inside and out. Watching her love for Abby was nothing short of inspirational and mesmerizing. Learning about her past and how far she'd come rocketed her into a whole new stratosphere of respect.

"What is it?" Grooves deepened on her forehead as those sky blue eyes penetrated his armor.

He started to speak but no words came. She seemed to understand as she walked straight to him and sat down on his lap. Her leggings and T-shirt hugged her curves. Beads of water rolled down her neck.

He looped his arms around her waist as she turned to straddle him. No words seemed necessary as she brought her hands up to his face.

"I know you can't kiss me because of the investigation." She leaned forward. "But that doesn't mean I can't kiss you."

Cash started to protest but it would be half-hearted. He brought his mouth to hers and pressed his lips to hers with the feeling of being home.

With a groan, he deepened the kiss. Her soft pink lips tasted like heaven. Peppermint toothpaste filled his senses. Peppermint was his new favorite flavor.

Her tongue delved into his mouth as she scooted her sweet, round bottom closer to his length. The effect she had on him was instantaneous, and a force of its own. He pressed his palms to the soft curve of her lower back and she rocked back and forth as she moaned her pleasure.

Her fingers dug into his shoulders, her nails against his hot skin as she dropped them to his arms was pure sin on Sunday. A need so intense Cash could scarcely fathom it welled up. He dropped his hands to each side of her hips as she rocked a little more.

His pulse raced, matching the tempo of hers. Reason escaped him as blood flew south. He tried to convince himself that lack of oxygen to the brain wasn't enabling him to break the rules. The annoying voice in the back of his mind returned, though. Repeating the two words that had the power to stop him in his tracks. *Game changer.*

With enormous effort, he pulled back.

"Believe me when I say that I want this to happen more than you could possibly imagine." His words came out through labored breaths.

"Why stop then?" She managed to say through her own heaves.

He didn't immediately respond. He needed a minute to slow his heart rate, and another to convince himself he was doing the right thing. "My job, for one."

Her shoulders deflated with his cop-out. "You're not exactly forcing me to do anything. In case you haven't noticed, I've been the forward one."

"That's not an issue for me. I like it a little too much when you take the lead." This time, he looked her straight in the eye because she needed to know where he stood. "Here's the other thing and it's the most important one. I've come to realize that you wouldn't be a casual fling for me, Renee. And your life is complicated right now. I'd be in the way. Plus, you've already said you're not ready for anything more than friends. What would we be doing here?"

"Not sleeping." She stared at him for a long moment. "I'm sorry I basically attacked you but—"

"Come on. We both know I was a willing participant."

"Plus, I doubt anything between us could be less than mind blowing," she said in a tone of voice that implied he'd offended her. Damn. He hadn't meant to do that. But she was temptation on a stick and he needed to keep a handle on his attraction.

"You're not making this any easier on me." He wanted nothing more than to block out the rest of the world and get lost with Renee even if it was for only a few hours. Once would never be enough with her. He'd want more and wouldn't be able to give it.

"You are right about one thing. My life is complicated." She climbed off his lap and sat on the bed. Her cheeks turned beet red and she toyed with the edge of the blanket. "I apologize for—"

"Don't. Believe me, you didn't hurt my feelings. You couldn't hurt my feelings if you tried. It's just not the play right now. You know?" He was doing a bad job explaining himself. "I know what I said before about not being ready to commit to anyone right now. But you're changing that for me. Being with you is a game changer. I don't know exactly what that means but I've never felt this way about anyone before you. If you decide you're ready for the possibility of something more…"

"You were right to stop things before they got out of control." The blush to her cheeks made him feel guilty.

"Being out of control with you would probably be one of my best days." His attempt at humor fell flat. If he'd met her a couple of years ago and she wasn't someone linked to his case, this would be a different situation. Kissing a beautiful woman was high on his list of things he enjoyed. But his heart wouldn't appreciate being stomped on as she walked out the door.

Damn. Was that the real reason he'd stopped her?

Cash forced the question aside and glanced at the clock. "All kidding aside, the little one won't be asleep much longer. I'm here. I'll probably just sleep on the chair. You can go to bed."

Now she really did laugh. "I'm betting that I'll be safe on the bed *with* you on it. You haven't slept in longer than me. You might as well claim the spot right here." She patted the pillow. "I promise to keep my hands to myself."

What she said was meant to be a joke, but Cash couldn't bring himself to laugh. In fact, there was nothing about her promise to leave him alone he thought was funny. How was that for proof that his priorities were upside-down?

"I probably won't be able to sleep, but I'm going to give it a shot anyway." She curled on her side on top of the covers, so he cut off the light.

Getting in bed with her was a bad idea. Instead, he waited until he heard her soft, steady breathing before easing his weight off the chair and heading toward the bathroom. A quick, cold shower woke him up. Damn good thing because he needed to be able to think clearly.

Cash walked over to the bassinet to check on the sleeping baby. Once he knew Abby was good, he returned to the chair and sat down. His head wasn't throbbing anymore, but it wouldn't hurt to close his eyes for a second or two.

The next thing he knew, the room was filled with light. He snapped his head up and glanced around. He rubbed his blurry eyes, looked down and saw that Renee had covered him with a blanket.

"Good morning." Her honey voice washed over him. She was sitting on the floor with a blanket spread out, playing with Abby.

"Morning," he grumbled. "I need coffee. Can I bring you a cup?"

"Already got one." She nodded toward the mug on the dresser.

A smile formed on his lips. He liked the fact she'd made herself comfortable at the ranch. "Baby's fed?"

"Fed, bathed and changed."

"How long was I out?" He checked the clock.

"Not too long. The minute she moved, I picked her up because I didn't want her to disturb you."

"I'm usually a light sleeper." He raked his hand through his hair.

"You needed the rest." There'd be no argument there.

"How about breakfast? Did you eat?" He needed to grab coffee for himself and, at the very least, a piece of toast.

She shot him a look. "Now that you mention it, I didn't eat. Any chance you have something light in the kitchen? Yogurt? A banana?"

"Do you like eggs and bacon?"

"Oh, bacon. Who doesn't love bacon?"

"How about a refresh on the coffee?" He walked over to the dresser to pick up her mug after she smiled and nodded.

"You should also know that once your mother found out about my tech skills, she offered me a job here."

Cash liked the sound of that a little too much.

"Did you take it?" He tried to sound casual.

"It's tempting. I told her that I'd think about it."

RENEE WAS IN serious trouble when it came to Cash. He had that whole ruggedly handsome bit down pat. He was also thoughtful and kind, and strong. She'd blinked her eyes open to see him checking on Abby last night and then pretended to be asleep. Her heart was pure liquid butter in her chest at the sight of him looking after her daughter.

To say she liked talking to him was a lot like

saying beef came from cows. Looking back, it was strange to think how bad things got between her and Jamison before she'd decided to call it quits. The decision had been so hard at the time and now she only wished she'd done it years ago.

How many times had she read a book or disappeared into the bedroom to avoid having a conversation with Jamison in recent years, and especially the last three or four? More than she could count.

In fact, it had become her habit. She'd listen to him talk about his day, smiling and nodding as he went into great detail about his general frustrations or his problems with a client. And when he was done, he would grab a beer and head off to watch football in the other room or spend time in front of the TV or on his laptop.

Early on, he'd been more attentive. There'd been a lot more shine on their relationship. The fact that he'd been the main topic of conversation hadn't bothered her in the beginning. She'd chalked it up to the fact that he was more of a talker than her instead of what became obvious to her later. He was self-absorbed. Jamison could be a charmer when he wanted to be, and especially when the relationship was new.

But that part of her life was moving into the past now. Renee took in a deep breath as she looked down at her daughter, the future. The little girl was happily cooing and talking the language Renee was certain only other babies understood.

Being here at the ranch with Cash and her daughter, her crazy, mixed-up world had righted itself. Even if it was for only a short time, she'd take it and then figure out how to make more of it. This was the feeling she wanted her daughter to grow up surrounded by. This felt a lot like unconditional acceptance…love?

Renee wasn't kidding about Margaret offering the job. The crazy part was that Renee was actually considering taking her up on it. Her boss had been understanding when Renee had spoken to her after the police. She'd asked for a few days and Rikki had agreed to them. But she wasn't known for being flexible with time off and having a baby was shifting Renee's priorities. She needed a steady job but she also wanted the flexibility to be with her daughter when she needed.

For now, her thoughts couldn't go in the direction of having anything more with Cash. Logic said they'd known each other only a short time. Her heart tried to argue differently because she'd taken it slow with Jamison and look where that had ended up. They'd been together for years and still hadn't made the marriage leap, a thought she was thankful for now.

Renee's cell dinged. She moved to her purse and checked the screen. Her battery was getting low. She needed to charge it.

The text caused her pulse to skyrocket.

Hey. Are you okay?

It was from Jamison. Why would he reach out to her while on his babymoon? Not that she believed any of it.

Should she respond? Technically, he was a suspect. Cash had said that Jamison's alibi was weak. Nothing in her wanted to have been in a relationship with someone who could want to hurt her, but she couldn't ignore the fact that he might want to take her daughter away. Kidnapping her newly adopted child ranked right up there with one of the worst offenses she could think of.

A thought struck her as odd. He asked about her and didn't mention Abby.

Cash walked into the room. She blinked up at him. His expression morphed to concern the second he looked at her. "What's wrong?"

She held her phone up, palm out. "Jamison just reached out to me."

Cash brought her plate of food and handed

over her coffee mug that he'd been balancing. "What did he say?"

"He asked if I'm okay."

Cash grunted. "He's letting you know that he's aware of your situation and trying to come off like he cares."

"The only person Jamison King cares about is himself." Shouldn't he be worried about his pregnant girlfriend? The fact that he'd landed squarely in the middle of a kidnapping investigation was most likely stressful for Yolanda. The fact the woman had had an affair with Jamison while he was still living with Renee didn't exactly rank high in her book, but he should still be focusing on her and not on Renee. "I'm not answering it."

"Maybe you should." He put his hand up to stop her from arguing. "Hear me out before you decide."

She nodded but he was walking into scary territory.

"I'd like to set up a meeting. Colton would be involved and you'd be nowhere near the scene. He's set up a sting before. That way, we could draw him out so he can be picked up for questioning." The way he put it made it sound like the risks would be nonexistent and she had no doubt Cash wouldn't put her in an unsafe environment.

"If he's behind the attempt, I'm still trying to figure out how he knew where I was moving and the fact that I'd adopted Abby. I kept that information close to my chest."

"Did he ever know your password to your laptop or your phone?" He quirked a brow.

"No." Well. Hold on a minute. She thought about the time he'd said he needed to check her inbox for a message from his mother's doctor. "Now that you mention it, I'm realizing that he did ask for my password a while back. But that was a long time ago. He said he needed to check my inbox because he'd given my email by mistake to the doctor's office where his mother was a patient. He asked them to send a referral. I can't remember how long ago it was. That whole time period toward the end is fuzzy. It was a year ago, maybe?" She shook her head to jog her memory. "I guess I forgot about him asking because I immediately changed my password that night."

Cash's eyebrow formed a perfect arch. "You didn't trust him?"

"Not after I found him checking my calendar early in our relationship and then questioning me about where I'd been and who I'd gone somewhere with." More red flags that Jamison was a jerk.

"Controlling men often install spy apps. All

he would've needed was a window of opportunity to infect your system." Cash's lips formed a thin line.

She should have suspected him more. She'd been too trusting and he'd become way too possessive. His mother's illness had changed him, amplified his bad qualities. Made him more self-absorbed. And angry. If he caught anyone talking to her at the office longer than he thought was appropriate, he'd fly off the handle with her later.

"Installing spyware would've been easy enough to do." She bit back a curse as she thought back to the few times that he seemed to slip. Looking back, there'd been the time when she'd told him that she was meeting one of the consultants for lunch and he'd dismissively told her that he knew that already. He'd saved his slipup by convincing her that she'd told him that morning, which was odd. She'd specifically remembered telling him that she'd been planning to meet with Rikki.

He'd made a joke about her being so busy that she was forgetting what she told him and what she didn't. Considering all the stress she'd been under trying to organize the move to Katy Gulch, she'd believed him.

How long had he known about her plans to adopt Abby? How long had he realized she was leaving him before she'd mentioned it? A hollow feeling expanded in her chest.

"I need to get Colton on the line." Cash's cell was already in hand but he seemed to be waiting for her to give a nod of approval. His thoughtfulness was foreign territory and she wanted to tread lightly. Her heart seemed to have other ideas when it fluttered wildly against her ribs. Cash was strong and considerate. He never seemed to feel the need to throw his weight around or force someone to do or say something they didn't want to.

"The guy from the lot was paid to bring his friends and scare me." She bit down on her bottom lip. "Why?"

"It could've been to throw the investigation off track." He'd said that before.

"The second attempt was very public," she said.

"Which could send a message that he can reach you anytime and in any place." He made good points—points that she hadn't thought about.

Cash's cell buzzed while still in his hand. He checked the screen and looked up. "It's Colton. He wants us to come to his office. Yolanda is in a fight with Jamison and just recanted her babymoon statement."

Chapter Seventeen

There was no way that Cash was going to ask Renee to leave Abby at the ranch, even though he thought it was the safest idea. She was determined to protect her daughter at all costs and would never leave her that long. He couldn't blame her.

"How long will it take to get her ready?" he asked.

"I just need a minute to put on real clothes." With that, Renee was up and rummaging through her weekend bag. She glanced at Abby and then him. His damn heart skipped a few beats, and he knew he was in deep water. He'd been in trouble from the minute he set eyes on her and figured he was just beginning to see the depths of where that was taking him.

Renee stepped out of the bathroom in a summer dress that bared the skin of her shoulders. Cash hadn't realized just how sexy shoulders could be until he'd seen her exposed. He tamped down his attraction and helped pack up a few supplies for Abby.

Within five minutes, the three of them were inside his vehicle and on their way down the country road leading to town.

"The car seems to put Abby at ease," he noticed. The ride to Colton's office had put the babbling baby to sleep. It had been the same with the twins.

"I love learning these little things about her." Renee smiled and more of that annoying warmth settled over him. There was a wistfulness to her tone and Cash realized that it most likely had to do with the possibility of losing the little girl who had already won Renee's heart. If the abduction attempt had been orchestrated by Kipp McGee or was somehow tied to Ms. Hubert, the possibility couldn't be ignored. But this case was looking more personal.

Cash realized he'd white-knuckled the steering wheel as he pulled into a parking spot at his brother's office. Renee was out of the passenger door before he could get around to her side, so he held open the back door as she unlocked the carrier from its base.

Cash leaned in and took the bag from the floorboard. He shouldered the strap and closed the door behind them.

Walking into the building, he caught their reflection in the glass door. Renee with Abby and him looking about as domestic as they come, a diaper bag over his right shoulder. It was like a lightning strike that packed a punch straight to the chest when he realized they made a damn fine-looking family.

She'd been clear on where she stood and he respected her position. Since those thoughts were about as productive as trying to get milk from a turnip, he shoved them aside.

Was he attracted to Renee? The answer to that question was a hard yes. To say the possibility of a relationship was complicated was an understatement.

His momentary shock at the realization they looked like a family was mirrored in his brother's expression the second the three of them walked into Colton's office.

"Good morning." Colton did a great job of hiding his thoughts but Cash knew his brother too well to let anything slide.

"Morning," Cash grumbled before pulling his brother into a hug. After Renee greeted Colton, he got right down to business.

"Ms. Tran is in the interview room, waiting. She got here ten minutes ago and has done nothing but pace the floor ever since." Colton shot a sympathetic look toward Renee. "Have you seen her in her present condition?"

Renee blinked. "Do you mean pregnant?"

Colton nodded.

"No."

"Is that something you're ready to—"

"The way my relationship with Jamison ended wasn't good, but I'm not in love with him." And then she added quietly, "I'm not certain that I ever was and any feelings I might have had died a long time ago."

Cash set his personal feelings aside and tried not to be too transparent about how happy those words made him. They made no difference to the case and that was all he needed to focus on. But Colton needed to know about the text she'd received earlier and he hadn't had a chance to bring his brother up-to-date yet. He glanced at Renee and their gazes locked for a second longer than they should've.

Colton caught the look between them.

"Jamison reached out to me this morning on my phone, asking if I was okay," she said.

"Text or phone call?" Colton asked.

"Text." Her gaze darted to her purse. "My phone is in here if you can grab it." She looked to Cash.

Without hesitating, he reached into her handbag and produced the cell, handing it over to his brother.

"I can unlock it with my thumbprint." Her

eyes widened. "My thumbprint." She repeated the words again. "He could've used my thumbprint when I was asleep, couldn't he? Before Abby, I slept like a rock. Now, I doubt I'll sleep until she's eighteen. Point being, he could've pressed my phone to my thumb at any time during the night to gain access to my emails."

Cash rocked his head. He didn't want to think about Renee being with the kind of jerk who would do something like that. In his line of work, he heard about scenarios like this more than he cared to. A jealous boyfriend or spouse could go to some pretty damn drastic lengths to keep tabs on a person. How they felt justified in doing so, Cash would never know or understand.

"A lot more about his behavior makes sense now from the past year." Renee's cheeks flamed when she got angry. She glanced at her daughter. She seemed to decide not to spit out the few choice words that were on the tip of her tongue.

A person like Renee came around once in a lifetime. Only an idiot would blow his chance with her if he was lucky enough to get one. And only a complete asshat would take advantage of her loyalty and devotion. Jamison King must not realize the value of those traits in a person.

"She was planning to give you a heads-up when we got the text to come here. Figured it was easy enough to tell you in person," Cash said to his brother.

"Mr. King reaching out to you is interesting considering the timing of his very pregnant girlfriend showing up in my office." Colton cocked his head to one side.

"I thought so, too." Cash couldn't agree more.

"I'm even more interested to hear what Ms. Tran has to say now." Colton's gaze bounced from Renee to Cash. "Shall we?"

With her lips forming a thin line, Renee nodded. If steam could come out of her ears, it probably would.

The betrayal was bad enough. Having to stand across the mirror from the evidence of it would devastate most people. Renee was strong, which didn't mean she wasn't suffering. Cash could see it in the tiny stress cracks around those clear blue eyes of hers.

Instinctively, he put his hand on the small of her back as they walked toward a person who she wouldn't be able to easily shut out of her mind when she closed her eyes that night.

Being done with her ex was a good thing. The bastard deserved to be strung up by his heels and left in the hot sun a day or two. Betrayal hurt. It stuck around. It festered if left to languish. He should know.

Betrayal, Cash understood.

Colton stopped in front of the viewing room. "Will you be okay in here?"

WHETHER OR NOT Renee was okay seemed to be the question of the day. For the record, she was not okay. She might never be okay again. But it had little to do with a very pregnant Yolanda Tran and Renee's ex.

The sad fact was she now hoped Jamison was responsible because that would mean her adoption couldn't be revoked.

Renee settled Abby's carrier on the seat of a chair, wedging the plastic in between the arm rests to keep her daughter's carrier secure.

The feeling of betrayal should have overwhelmed her when she walked into the small, dimly lit room adjacent to the interview room. Yolanda was beautiful. She had long, straight silky-black hair that fell to her waist. She had a round face with dark brown eyes. She was a tiny thing except for the big belly announcing to the world that she was carrying a child.

Instead of betrayal, Renee felt closure.

The woman, who was pacing around the room, worked her hands together. Her fingers laced and then she balled a hand. It seemed like she couldn't be still in any part of her body. The stress of being with a man like Jamison, who could be so charming until he wasn't, was written all over her actions and especially all over her face.

The all-too-familiar stress that Renee had felt at being with a man who ignored everyone else's feelings and thought only about himself. Yeah, Renee recognized that look in Yolanda because she'd stared at it in the mirror once. It was the reason she'd decided to leave and start over.

Watching Yolanda was just the reminder Renee needed. Jamison was a coward and a jerk.

Although Yolanda's morals were seriously off to have an affair with a man she knew was in a relationship, Renee felt nothing but pity for the woman who would have Jamison's child in a matter of weeks.

"I should probably hate her," she whispered to Cash, who stood right beside her. "I can't."

He studied Yolanda for a long moment. "She looks like she's carrying the weight of the world on her shoulders."

"It was the same for me at the end and the reason I finally walked away. Makes me kind of stupid, doesn't it?" She barely finished her sentence and he was already shaking his head.

"Caring about someone else doesn't make you stupid. It makes you human. Making a mistake does the same thing. Besides, you would've left the jerk a long time ago if his mother hadn't been sick, and he sounds like a master manipulator." Every word of what he'd just said was true.

"It's hard not to feel like a sucker." Admitting it, saying the words out loud made them lose some of their power. She'd been so embarrassed that she'd let the relationship go for so long without breaking up that she'd been quiet. Then again, the only person she ever really talked to was her boss, who'd always encouraged Renee to stick it out with Jamison. Renee didn't have the first idea why she'd listened to Rikki.

"Being loyal to someone doesn't make you bad." Cash turned toward her, his strong body standing within inches of her. He brought his hands up to her face and cupped her cheeks. "Your ex was the idiot. He doesn't deserve you." And then under his breath, he said, "If you were with me, I'd know how to treat you."

Renee's pulse skyrocketed and her stomach free-fell. She pushed up to her tiptoes and pressed her lips to his. Bringing her hands up, she dug her fingers into his shoulders.

Voices coming through the speaker shocked them back a step.

"Ms. Tran, my name is Sheriff Colton O'Connor. We spoke on the phone." Colton walked over to her and extended his right hand.

She accepted the offering. Her face was sheet white.

"I'm not sure if I should even be here." Her hand dropped down to cradle her stomach as she surveyed the room.

Anger toward Jamison was a flame inching toward a dry field in the middle of a draught. The thought a child would be caught in the middle made Renee burn.

Colton gave Yolanda a look that Renee figured was meant to reassure Yolanda. Being so stressed while pregnant couldn't be good for her or the baby. A couple of times in the last few minutes, the woman's face tensed and she seemed like she was blowing air slowly out of her mouth like she had a cramp.

"Would you like to sit down?" Colton motioned toward the chairs. He seemed to catch on, too. The chairs had been moved from across the table to one side. The arrangement seemed more intimate and less confronting.

Interesting.

"No, thank you." Yolanda wasn't done pacing. She brought her hands to her hips. Anyone could see that she was debating walking out the door and taking her information with her.

"How about you talk to me a little bit about why you're here." Colton's voice was steady. Renee assumed it was meant to keep Yolanda calm and it seemed to be working when she blew out a slow breath.

She chewed on her lip, seemed to be reconsidering stopping in.

"I don't have to remind you that lying to an officer of the law counts as impeding an investigation. You could be held in contempt. Jailed."

She gasped.

"It's not too late for you to make it right. Tell me what brought you here and what part of your earlier statement you're recanting." Colton crossed his arms over his chest.

A few seconds that felt like minutes passed by without her opening her mouth.

"A baby was almost kidnapped." Colton's gaze dropped to her belly where she was cradling her bump.

"I'm sorry about that. I can't help you after all." She took a step toward the exit.

"Walk out that door and I find out that you lied there'll be trouble at your door in a heartbeat."

"I didn't do anything wrong." She froze.

"If you're covering for someone who did, you could go to jail as an accomplice." Those words got the tears rolling. She was teetering on a ledge. Renee hoped the woman would tip over. As awful as it was, Jamison trying to kidnap Abby was so much better than a botched adoption. It could've been one of his friends that first night. With Jamison, it was personal.

Yolanda's expression dropped and more tears came flooding. "He told me to say he was with me, but he wasn't. I don't know where he was, who he was with or where he's been but he told me his ex was trying to frame him for something he didn't do. I had no idea there was a child involved. He… He…"

She broke down crying and it was difficult for Renee not to force her way into the adjacent room and try to offer some comfort to the woman. At the very least for the child's sake. Colton picked up the box of tissues from the table and offered them to Yolanda.

"Do you know where Jamison King is right now?" Colton asked when the tears stemmed.

"No, I don't. We've been in a hotel room off the highway. We had a huge fight because I wanted to go home and he told me that he didn't want to have this baby with me. He said that I wasn't anything like his ex and that he still loved her. He was always comparing me to her during our relationship. Renee this and Renee that. He talked about how perfect she was. At first, I accepted it because…" She hesitated long enough to wipe a few more tears. "I knew he was still with her when we started dating. He convinced me that it had been over between the two of them for a long time but that he didn't want to leave her with everything happening with his mother. Renee loved his mother."

"That's news to me." Renee nearly choked hearing those words. Renee had never really gotten along with the woman.

"I thought maybe he'd gone back to her when I found out she was near. My boss left a few messages saying he'd talked to a sheriff." Was Yolanda trying to get back at him for leaving? Despite feeling sorry for her, Renee wouldn't trust that woman as far as she could throw her. And, yes, the tears got to Renee. It was difficult seeing a pregnant woman so upset.

"We'd like to talk to Mr. King if you see him or if he contacts you." Colton was a study in calm.

"I can't believe he'd do anything to break the law. I thought I knew him better than that," Yolanda said.

Renee coughed. Seriously?

Yolanda cradled her bump and Renee wasn't sure how much of that was now being played for sympathy.

"She sure likes to remind my brother that she's pregnant," Cash said low and under his breath.

"You noticed that, too?" Of course he would

in his line of work. Renee wasn't used to being around someone so observant.

"That's probably the fifth time she's made a show of touching her bump," he noted.

"At least." The air seemed to thin and breathing was difficult. "I need to take a walk. Get some air. If I look at this show anymore, I might lose my temper." Renee glanced at her angel who was still sleeping in the carrier. "Will you keep an eye on her for a minute?"

Cash looked like he was trying to make a decision. Then came, "Yeah, sure. Do me a favor, though?"

"Name it."

"Stay at the front door where Gert can see you at all times." A chill raced down her spine at the reminder of the danger she was in.

"Deal."

This time, it was Cash who hauled her against his chest. He pressed his lips to hers. "Good. I can't have anything happening to you."

Didn't those words melt what was left of Renee's resolve. Logistics be damned, she was starting to believe she could open her heart a little more to Cash. She *wanted* to.

"I'm safe as long as I'm with you."

He pressed a slow, sweet kiss to her lips before stepping back and refocusing on the witness.

Renee walked out of the room, down the hall

and past Gert's desk. She was on the phone but she glanced up and waved. Renee pointed to the front door and Gert nodded.

There was no amount of time that could erase the damage that Jamison had done to their relationship. Seeing his new girlfriend pregnant with his child was a slap of reality—one she needed. Caring for Jamison wasn't the problem. Those feelings were long gone. Seeing him ruin another person's life and bring a child into the world when he'd been clear that he never wanted children set the blaze. The child deserved better. Every child deserved better.

As Renee walked the sidewalk in front of the building, the devil himself walked up from behind her.

"I thought I'd never get you alone again." Those were the last words she heard before a blow to the head caused her world to go black.

Chapter Eighteen

Renee blinked her eyes open. Jamison was shoving her into the back of his car. He was trying to force something over her mouth. A cloth? There was a smell she didn't recognize but it was strong. She tried to scream. He grabbed her by the throat cutting off her voice.

When did he become this strong? He squeezed so hard she thought her eyeballs might pop out. Drawing up her knees, she pulled on all the strength she could muster and kicked with everything she had inside her.

There was enough force to knock him back a step and loosen the grip.

"No." He bit the word out with so much anger. "You don't get to leave me again, Renee. Ever. I was just trying to scare you into coming home but you won't scare. You don't need a child, Renee. She's in the way. You need me."

"I don't love you, Jamison," was all she managed to say before his hand was back on her throat.

Kicking and screaming—her cries were muffled—she unleashed hell on him.

"You forgot how much you love me. It'll come back or you'll love no one. I sure as hell won't let you stay with that cowboy." He tightened his grip as she dug her fingernails into his hand.

During the struggle, she'd lost her glasses and all she could see was a blurry mess in front of her, on top of her. Despite her efforts, she couldn't make him budge.

She scratched his face, digging her nails into his cheeks deep enough to break the skin.

"You shouldn't do that, Renee." He tightened his grip until she thought she might black out again.

With all her energy, she twisted and rolled onto her side. She landed hard on the floorboard but at least managed to break his choke hold. He came down on top of her and she felt his hands struggling for purchase. Despite the fact her windpipe hurt and she gasped for air, she managed to buck him off.

"Cash." She screamed the word, praying someone would hear her. It was broad daylight. The statistic that most women were abducted under these conditions came to mind. It was high.

Not her, not if she had anything to say about it.

Suddenly, Jamison's weight was ripped off her. She heard a voice—Cash's voice—giving her the first sign of hope.

Scrambling to her feet, she managed to get out of the car on her own. Her throat hurt and she couldn't count the number of bruises forming on her skin but she could feel every one.

"Cash." He was a blur but she would recognize him anywhere. She fumbled around for her glasses and found them. When she put them on, she looked in time to see Cash's fist rear back before landing a punch that caused Jamison's head to snap back.

Blood shot from his nose as Cash made quick work of tackling Jamison to the cement, face first.

"You're going to spend the rest of your life in jail if I have anything to say about it." Cash rammed his knee into Jamison's back, holding him in place while Colton pulled zip cuffs from his belt and then cuffed him.

The second Jamison was secure, Cash closed the distance between him and Renee in a few strides. She saw the worry lines scoring his forehead.

"I thought I lost you." He cupped her face in his hands and searched her eyes.

"I'm okay, Cash. I'm here. Safe. Where's Abby?" She glanced around, frantic.

"Gert's bringing her out. She didn't want the little girl anywhere near Jamison."

Renee pushed up to her tiptoes and kissed him.

"What about Kipp McGee and the adoption?" she asked when she pulled back.

"He might be tied to the Hubert case, but he's not involved here, which means this adoption is real," Cash said.

"I've never believed in love at first sight," Renee said to Cash after everything settled down and they were alone in Colton's office. "I wouldn't know how to trust it."

"Really?" He looked at Abby. "Because I don't believe you. How long did it take for you to realize you would make any sacrifice for Abby? Did you know her?"

"In my heart, I knew her all along. Meeting her was the next logical step," she said without hesitation.

"When it came to Abby, you let your feelings take the lead. You didn't question them or put up a wall." He wasn't sure if he was getting through to Renee, but he had to try. "I'm not saying what we have is the same as a love for a child, don't get me wrong. The two are very different animals. Since I met you, I became a believer in love at first sight. I knew you were going to be important to me from the minute you opened the door and I stood on your porch. I just didn't know how. It would be a shame not to see where that takes us because I've never experienced a lightning bolt like that with anyone else. If you don't feel the same way, I'll walk out the door and leave you alone. Say the word and I'm gone."

She was making quick work of the baby cloth in her hand. Her head was tilted to one side and he could see how much she was chewing on his words. He meant every one of them. All she had to do was tell him to walk. He'd hate it. But he'd respect her wishes.

"What if I said that I do want to spend more time together, but life is in the way right now. I have Abby to think about. I can't exactly see myself leaving her with a babysitter. Relationships take time. Getting to know each other takes time."

"If someone had said the same thing to me last week, I would've agreed."

Renee took in a deep breath. She usually did that when she was fortifying herself to say something that was difficult or face a new challenge. He had no idea which way she would go on this one. All he knew for certain was that her words would either open a door or close one. With Renee, she would go all in or walk away.

"I knew you were special the minute I saw you. I had no idea what that meant until you stepped up time and time again for me and my daughter. I should probably be afraid of my feelings for you. You have the power to shatter me, Cash." There was so much vulnerability in her words and he could see that it was taking great effort for her to admit her feelings. "So, don't."

"Does this mean what I think it does? You'll give us a chance?" Hope ballooned in his chest.

"No."

That one word had the power to devastate him.

She continued before he could respond. "A chance implies there's an option to fail. I love you. I've known it since the second we met. I want to run toward it instead of reason my way out. Because it's clear to me that I'll never find someone who fits me in the way you do. I'll never find someone who makes my heart flutter and yet still makes me feel safe even though I'm risking all I have, all that I am. I choose you."

"In that case." Cash took her hand in his and dropped down on one knee. "Let's make it permanent. Let's start our family today and not look back. I love you, Renee. I'm never going to find someone who challenges me to be the best person I can be like you do. I've never been so in love before I met you. You're it for me and I want the world to know. I want to adopt Abby and make our family official in the eyes of the law. I want our little girl to have every right afforded an O'Connor. We can proceed any way you like. But, if you'll have me, I'd be honored if you'll agree to marry me."

"Yes, Cash. I'll marry you. With all my heart, I'll marry you."

With those words, he stood and brought her into his arms.

She blinked at him and said, "I can't wait to make our family official but I don't need a piece of paper to know what's in my heart. You're my family and I can't imagine a better father for Abby."

"The kid struck gold when she landed you as a mother," he countered. "Both of you won my heart. And, now, I'm ready to build a life together."

"I can't think of a better way to spend the next fifty or sixty years than with you and our daughter." When she looked at him, her eyes sparked. "And maybe a couple of siblings for Abby."

"My job in law enforcement is important to me for now. I'm not ready to give it up. Are you okay with that?" he asked.

"Don't ever change for me. I love you for who you are. When and if you're ever ready to take more responsibility at the ranch, I'll support that decision."

He looked at her and his chest nearly burst with love and pride. He kissed her, slow and sweet.

"My mother has offered you a job at the ranch. Any chance you'd consider taking her up on it? You'd be an asset on the ranch, especially with your technical abilities. What do you think about helping her run the place? KBR is as much yours as it is my brothers', mine and Abby's."

Renee beamed. "I'd like to use my skills to continue the legacy we'll hand down to our children. So, that's a yes from me."

"I love you, Renee." With those words, Cash found home.

Epilogue

The open door to Mother's library stopped Cash in the hallway. It was early, even for her.

A light was on, telling him she was inside. She always made a point to walk through the house before bed and turn off lights. She called it putting the house to bed and told him even the house needed to rest.

Taking in a deep breath, he took the couple of steps until he stood in front of the door.

"Morning." Her voice cracked enough to let him know she'd been crying. Crying wasn't something he'd seen his mother do very often.

"Hello, beautiful. What are you doing up at this hour?" He wished he could reel the question back in the minute he'd asked it. She was grieving and, based on the fact she had her favorite book in her hand, searching for comfort.

She held up the worn paperback.

"Mind if I join you?" There was something about her expression that made him want to stick around a few minutes. See if he could provide some comfort to the woman who'd spent most of her life taking care of him and his brothers. How did he even begin to repay the kind of loyalty and dedication she'd shown to him and his brothers?

"Please do." The warmth in his mother's eyes returned. Thinking about taking care of Abby and the weight of the responsibility ahead of him—responsibility he gladly took on even though he was way out of his league—made him appreciate everything his parents had done for him and his brothers. It also made him resolve to clear the air with Garrett. Losing their father made Cash realize how important family was and how much he'd taken for granted that they'd all be there. Wounds could be healed *someday*. Time would wait for them to catch up.

Flawed thinking. A little voice in the back of his mind said the best way to honor his father's memory was to pass on his unconditional love, his easygoing nature and his unwavering belief in his children. That same voice reminded Cash that his investigative work wasn't done. Not until Caroline's story was told, not until he gave his mother closure, whatever that meant—and that might mean delivering news no son wanted to give his mother in a case like this.

"I don't have many regrets with your father," his mother started after he claimed a seat. "We had a beautiful marriage. Not perfect, mind you. But it was better than I ever dreamed possible considering I never saw my parents show affection one time. I think they came from a generation of 'united front' mindset."

He chuckled. His grandparents had been stiff people. He couldn't remember a time when his grandmother wasn't dressed to the nines, wearing her pearls, sipping tea from a delicate cup. "Remember when I poured Nana's tea into a coffee mug once?"

Margaret laughed. "I thought she would have a heart attack."

"But she was too proper to scold me."

"Her back went straighter than a board." Margaret slapped her hands together. It felt good to make her laugh. Damned if she didn't deserve to smile again. Grief would be a cloud over her, the ranch, for a while. There was a time for grief and a time to laugh. He'd grab every happy moment he could. "But her face was priceless."

"Her lip was stiffer than the queen's."

Now, his mother really laughed and it was a musical sound.

"What about Ruth Hubert?" Margaret leaned forward and her serious expression returned.

"Remains to be seen." He needed to set realistic expectations. "It'll most likely take time to unravel that tangled mess."

"Her files?"

"They'll take a while to unpack." Cash knew exactly what his mother was asking. Could Ms. Hubert possibly be connected to Caroline's disappearance?

Time would tell.

"Abby's adoption?" she asked.

"Is legitimate. Colton will be working with the feds on the Hubert adoption ring. We won't give up until we find out if she had anything to do with Caroline's case." He looked at his mother, who was surrounded by her books in the library. He wished he could give her the answers she needed.

"You got hold of Garrett." She smiled.

"He's coming." Cash nodded.

"Your father wouldn't want me to be sad." She had that part right.

"No. He wouldn't."

"He wouldn't want you to be, either."

"It's hard not to miss him." Another point there was no argument for. "He left big shoes to fill."

Margaret clucked her tongue. "You've always been your own person, Cash. Your father wouldn't want it any other way. He would never expect you to become him in any way and that means working here at the ranch. You can do anything you want, be anything you want."

"My place is here. I *want* to be here and take my place on the ranch. What you guys built here should be carried forward for—"

She held up her hand to stop him. "You love your job. It's important to do work that you feel passionate about."

"I love this, too." He nodded in the direction of the backyard. There was one case that he hadn't solved and it was his reason to go to work every day. "I'm not ready to give up my job just yet. Make no mistake about it, this is my home. This ranch, this land is exactly where I belong. This is ultimately where my heart says I should be. I've never been more certain of anything in my life."

Cash looked for a sign of disapproval or acceptance in his mother's face. She gave no hint of her feelings. When he really thought about it, she'd always been there for him. Never judging him. Always making him feel like he couldn't go wrong. He thought about Abby and how ready he was to become her father. The fact that he even wanted kids at all was news to him. The little girl held special magic in her smile if it made him want to sign on to parenthood.

But then, she was special. She deserved parents who gave her the same kind of unconditional love Cash had grown up with.

"Take your time. A place will always be here

waiting for you," his mother said and he realized she'd been studying him.

"The only thing I know for certain right now is that I want to make Renee my wife and adopt Abby."

His mother beamed. "I like her a lot." She paused. "She accepted my job offer to work on the ranch."

"Seems like a good way to get to know the family business." In losing his father, Cash realized how very short time actually was in this life. Instead of it making him depressed, he saw it as a call to action.

"I want to be part of the business again and I don't want to wait. If we could take it slow for now and work up to me being here full-time one day, that would be ideal." He would come to his own in the family ranch. He wanted to be part of it. But not yet. He hadn't solved his biggest case yet.

But for now, he was focused on Renee and Abby. And that was enough.

* * * * *

Look for the next book in USA TODAY
bestselling author Barb Han's
An O'Connor Family Mystery miniseries
when Texas Target *goes on sale*
in November 2020!

Get 4 FREE REWARDS!

We'll send you 2 FREE Books <u>plus</u> 2 FREE Mystery Gifts.

Harlequin Presents books feature the glamorous lives of royals and billionaires in a world of exotic locations, where passion knows no bounds.

FREE
Value Over
$20

YES! Please send me 2 FREE Harlequin Presents novels and my 2 FREE gifts (gifts are worth about $10 retail). After receiving them, if I don't wish to receive any more books, I can return the shipping statement marked "cancel." If I don't cancel, I will receive 6 brand-new novels every month and be billed just $4.55 each for the regular-print edition or $5.80 each for the larger-print edition in the U.S., or $5.49 each for the regular-print edition or $5.99 each for the larger-print edition in Canada. That's a savings of at least 11% off the cover price! It's quite a bargain! Shipping and handling is just 50¢ per book in the U.S. and $1.25 per book in Canada.* I understand that accepting the 2 free books and gifts places me under no obligation to buy anything. I can always return a shipment and cancel at any time. The free books and gifts are mine to keep no matter what I decide.

Choose one: ☐ **Harlequin Presents Regular-Print** (106/306 HDN GNWY)   ☐ **Harlequin Presents Larger-Print** (176/376 HDN GNWY)

Name (please print)

Address   Apt. #

City   State/Province   Zip/Postal Code

Email: Please check this box ☐ if you would like to receive newsletters and promotional emails from Harlequin Enterprises ULC and its affiliates. You can unsubscribe anytime.

Mail to the **Reader Service:**
IN U.S.A.: P.O. Box 1341, Buffalo, NY 14240-8531
IN CANADA: P.O. Box 603, Fort Erie, Ontario L2A 5X3

Want to try 2 free books from another series! Call 1-800-873-8635 or visit www.ReaderService.com.

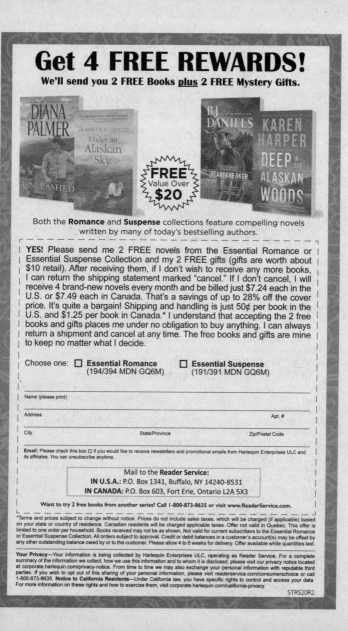

COMING NEXT MONTH FROM

H HARLEQUIN

INTRIGUE

Available October 27, 2020

#1959 ROOKIE INSTINCTS
Tactical Crime Division: Traverse City • by Carol Ericson

TCD team member Aria Calletti is determined to find out why women are turning up dead. The newest victim's half brother, Grayson Rhodes, has sacrificed everything to find his half sister and her son. But can a civilian and a new agent take down a drug kingpin?

#1960 TEXAS TARGET
An O'Connor Family Mystery • by Barb Han

After bailing Summer Grayson, his ex-wife's identical sister, out of jail, US marshal Dawson O'Connor agrees to help Summer, who is convinced her twin is in danger. He'll do anything to protect her, even as she ups the stakes by posing as her missing sibling.

#1961 CLOSE RANGE CHRISTMAS
A Badlands Cops Novel • by Nicole Helm

Dev Wyatt's worst fear has come true. Someone from the Wyatts' dangerous past is stalking his family—and his best friend, Sarah Knight, who is pregnant with his child. As Sarah and Dev battle escalating threats, will they survive long enough to become a family?

#1962 INVESTIGATION IN BLACK CANYON
The Ranger Brigade: Rocky Mountain Manhunt
by Cindi Myers

After Cara Mead's boss disappears in the wilderness, Cara enlists the help of Ranger Brigade officer Jason Beck. But once the manhunt is set in motion, Jason and Cara find themselves embroiled in a fearsome conspiracy—and someone will do anything to keep them from finding out the truth.

#1963 DANGEROUS KNOWLEDGE
Fortress Defense • by Julie Anne Lindsey

After investigative journalist Katlin Andrews is run off the road, she awakens with Fortress Defense bodyguard Jack Hale in her hospital room. He promised to protect his best friend's sister. With Katlin unable to recall who's after her, he'll have to use all his skills to stop an unseen threat.

#1964 HIGH-PRIORITY ASSET
A Hard Core Justice Thriller • by Juno Rushdan

When US marshal Dutch Haas enters Isabel Vargas's life to get information on her uncle, he knows she'll become his partner instead of his mark. With threats stacking up, will Isabel and Dutch be able to stop Isabel's past from catching up with her before it is too late?

YOU CAN FIND MORE INFORMATION ON UPCOMING HARLEQUIN TITLES,
FREE EXCERPTS AND MORE AT HARLEQUIN.COM.

HICNM1020